Only the Lover Sings

Daniel Fitzpatrick

En Route Books & Media, LLC
St. Louis, MO

Make the time

En Route Books and Media, LLC
5705 Rhodes Avenue
St. Louis, MO 63109

Cover credit: TJ Burdick

Library of Congress Control Number:
2020934844

ISBN-13: 978-1-952464-00-3

DEDICATION

for Grace

FOREWORD

In the wake of Hurricane Katrina, late in the autumn of 2005, when the best friend of my childhood told me of his conversion to atheism, I felt more clearly than ever prior or since the presence of nothing. And I had nothing to say. Ten years later, as I began to write *Only the Lover Sings*, it occurred to me that here, in conversation with nothing, I might mythologize the first part of my life. I take myth not simply as fanciful explanation of the natural but rather as man's creative attempt to situate himself between creation and the Creator. Thus, my seven chapters and their titles and the faint hope that in a return to the mythopoeic the [Catholic] novel might begin to be restored.

Those who know me will no doubt recognize the autobiographical elements contained herein. I ask them to remember Waugh's epigraph to *Brideshead Revisited*: "I am not I; thou art not he or she; they are not they." There is only One who knows myth from memory and memory from event; in Him all Scandal is perfected.

OVERTURES

It was during the summer before my wedding that I last spoke with Francis. Before then it had been three years since, with hardly a word, I'd embraced him briefly at my godmother's wake and wept into the long hair curling to his shoulders like winter tendrils and redolent even then of the memory of a sunlit bedroom and a half drunk bottle of Kentwood in the top bunk, of all those first eighteen years in New Orleans, of music's blooming discipline, of whispered lust and hatred, of belief and its loss and the swirling gravity of the storm. My family, clustered in the pews near the altar, had whispered and stared. We were both just twenty. In those three forgetful years between I'd texted him once, perhaps, on his birthday, and worse, called him soliciting donations for Ignatius Prep, where I was teaching Theology at the time. He hadn't answered, and I'd left an awkward message, and we hadn't spoken of it.

Only by chance or some ill-understood suggestion of providence had I arranged to meet him now. I had sent my grandmother a letter; it had been returned. Confused, I had laid it aside, though later in the day I'd realized that the number to which I'd addressed the missive was Francis's and not my grandmother's after all.

I hesitated to the end, three times raising my phone to cancel and three times replacing it in my pocket. I've since, with much the same feeling, watched certain bills accumulate on the counter in hope of vanquishing my creditors. So I suggested a sushi place where the chef waved as I walked in and the waitress always brought a free dessert. But the soup and rolls and ice cream passed in vain. Francis's hair was short again, but his voice, clear in memory, seemed to have retreated from his mouth and lodged deep in his throat. We had said nothing, and as we both wanted a coffee, we visited another of my Mid-City haunts, three blocks toward the lake from Ignatius. I'd spent most of my afternoons there, reading a flaking copy of Whitman and scribbling some glosses in verse and drinking cold coffee against my afternoon headaches. The notebook I carried then has since gone missing, and while most of it was best lost there was one short poem I miss now and then, a bit of free verse about a child Christ creeping into Joseph's shop and, catching a splinter in his finger, foreseeing the Cross for the first time. I've never had a hand for recreation, so I've left the idea alone, hoping the notebook should reemerge. I'm concerned my mother has hidden it away somewhere.

So we met again in the coffee shop, a dirty place, open as much to dogs as to people, where our soles stuck slightly at each step. A band of copper paint ran somewhere near the ceiling in memory. As usual the barista, a pale brunette whose hair hung defiantly in the same loose knot every day, set my drink at the bar as I reached it. Curious, she turned to Francis: "What would you like?"

His eyes moved blindly over the chalkboard menu above her.

Reddening, I turned to him: "Do you drink it the same?"

"Sure."

"I got it if you wanna grab us a table."

He chose a small table in the center of the cafe. A minute later, as I sat and handed him a spoon and a frozen golden concoction topped in whipped cream, he began.

"Sorry I never called you back."

I paused a moment. "Oh, it's fine. I felt bad calling you anyway."

"As you know, I didn't have the best time there."

"Yeah, it's fine; neither did I."

"So much hate. But mostly that they let us hate. Gay jokes, Jew jokes, woman jokes, whatever, and nobody ever saying anything about it."

"Do you think that's just boys?"

"I don't think it has to be. But people get to say things like 'I hate fags'--in Scripture class--and nobody does anything."

His voice rose to his tongue again, clear and impassioned, as it had sounded throughout our youth.

"Who was teaching?"

"Ruggi. He just let it go."

"When was that?"

"Freshman year--you were there."

"I don't remember that. Maybe I was sick...but yeah, for sure, he should have said something. I'd've torn into him. It's hard, though, because you start to see they're all just repeating what their parents say. That's what I've found hardest."

"I can see that. I just wish there could have been more of a dialogue. Like the time they made us write a prayer and I said I didn't pray and they said 'Well, you need it most of all'."

"Yeah, it's gotten a lot better since then. Theology has, anyway, much better than when we were there."

He stirred the whipped cream into his drink. After a moment I began again, "I hope...I never wanted to seem that way." I saw him once again, standing alone in the center aisle as the communicants passed and seating himself again alone at the end of the pew.

He frowned, shook his head slightly. "No, you were always very respectful."

"I always worried I drove you away somehow."

"No, it's just the way things happened, I think. And Ruggi."

We both laughed a moment as images of the old man, himself enormous and varied as Endymion, paraded across our minds; then we stilled as he vanished into the flood each felt he'd caused.

"I think there's a reason we all loved him, but I bet he'll have a lot to answer for."

Francis nodded. "Sometimes I wish he would have been a little less tolerant. Do you remember the day I stayed to talk to him after class?"

I felt the blood in my face. "Of course."

"I wanted to tell him why I was doubting. Do you know what he said?"

"Hm?"

"That I had good reasons. I mean, come on, I was fourteen. I might've listened if he'd said something."

I nodded, gazing intently at some point over his shoulder.

"I guess you still believe?"

"Much more than then, no thanks to me, I'm sure."

"Doesn't it all bother you?"

"More and more, but I think that's a part of why I believe it more."

I said a lot after that, most of it the kind of philosophical obfuscation I tend to fall back on like some hill there in plain sight that no one else seems to know. I remember there was a bit about Al-Ghazali and a lot about Hegel and identity-in-difference, just enough of the progressive edge in it all to keep comfortable and still feel I'd said something. I said a lot about love and felt the beady eyes of the neighborhood roosters upon me.

He listened appreciatively, added an approving word here and there. In the end he said simply, "I'm glad you're happy."

We both felt then that it was time to go, that we had gone nearly too far, almost crossed into some deeper commitment that each of us wanted but was too tired or busy or afraid to take up at the moment. We said as we walked out into the heavy July heat that we would keep in touch, maybe cook together some time. Then he hugged me and turned away toward the river, while I went on toward the lake and City Park. It was the last I saw of him save the wedding, no place to return to old intimacy.

There had been plenty of rain that year, and the oaks' verdant bosk blanketed me in shade as I crossed the few blocks to the park. The streetcars were full of thin tourists in light clothes, and through the heavy panicles of the crepe myrtles' six-month bloom I followed their progress past me, a blurred and indistinct feature of the shaded facades flickering before them. Soon I came level with the Mid-City welcome sign, the crimson heart nestled in the yellow crescent moon, and turned left along the bottom of the park. In the fields along the deep lagoons, moss-backed and black as tea, were scattered groups of women at aerobics, shirtless men gleaming in pursuit of frisbees, children frisking after dogs, their young skin impervious to the heat.

At the stone gates men and women in pastels and linen were whisked from their cars at the hands of maroon, sweating valets and into the cool natural light of Ralph's on the Park. I passed on, tasting sazerac and turtle soup and a fillet of drum I'd eaten many years before. The park was empty here and my steps slowed as hesitantly I gave myself to thought. Above in the overheated blue a gull laughed long and thin.

By the time I'd neared the edge of the park I'd settled on writing a note, another indirection centering on Heidegger and angst and nothing. Just as I prepared to cross Marconi, Francis's car jolted over its pockmarked face in front of me. He didn't see me, but my thoughts scattered and the blood jumped to my throat as though by chance I'd met a girl I'd hardly known I'd hoped to see.

I hurried on again, past the community college and the masonic cemetery into the bright, barren plain of graves along the interstate. I cut through one of them, Cypress Grove, with its one oak set back in a corner, its shaded roots littered with beer cans and candy wrappers and more dubious detritus. The heat and the highway thunder beat me on to the shelter of Banks Street and I slowed and slowed more beneath its arched oaks.

At the far end of the street rose Ignatius Prep once more to overpower me. I felt the terror of it then again as I had when first I'd entered its broad white halls. It was mostly empty, and I let myself in by a side door and rose by a brief brown flight of stairs to the small chapel.

The sun had gone far in its descent toward the sea, and the newly cleaned glass flamed its tales as I knelt in my usual place in the second pew. The cool air pressed the sweat against my back and into my groin and for a moment the discomfort was all. Then it gave way, first to the scent of varnish on the new cherry floors and then to the old feeling of failure and finally to the plain request to remind me that I am not.

I.

MAYBE EVEN THESE

And it was long before then, almost as long before as could be for him, and he lay staring into the galaxy of motes swirling down the light toward the green couch as a faint sickness crept over him. He wondered vaguely at the dust and the light and all that the light missed and at the image of his father bent over a vacuum or risen on tiptoe to brush a mounted bird's wing. And at length he rose and stepped through the thin wooden door with its loose lock and out into the humid Sun, so hot that he shivered as he did in descending to a bath, and he slipped through a gap between the grey board fence and the pink brick of the house and wandered past the neighbors' burnt-out forno and found himself in the green shade of the great live Oak. And being less afraid then he pored over the litter for some sign of the bright birds who summered in the canopy, the cardinal, the blue jay, the mockingbird and mourning dove, and never until he had discovered some bright symbol would he walk home, usually by way of the burning sidewalk, cracked here and again by the brooding oaks, and glide through the sticky Douglas firs that framed the front yard and back inside by the front door.

And he lay what feathers he'd found on a cedar desk his father had built and stood at his bedroom's south-facing window and watched the light accumulating in the clouds addled always by the breeding of the sun and the sea. And he wondered dimly at its woven wilderness except in this that seemed to unfold from west to east.

There were many more trees below the Sun then, many more than the oaks, knee-deep in water always already: the firs; the dusty, leathery magnolias; red maples; crepe myrtles, their paper skin riddled with massive black ants, dry and shining in the heat. Their shade lay in deep green continuous pools up and down the cracked black streets like summer streams over broken beds.

And always in the midst there flew the birds, the wheeling lines of gulls laughing high above, the hawks and the vultures perning in the afternoons, the mockingbird who set up every evening on the streetlamp in the oyster-shell alley and improvised above the garbage cans to the dull thundering sostenuto of the interstate and the shrieking punctuations of the freight trains. The sound of engines blended forever with the words of his drifting prayers which since he'd turned five had always ended "and please let us all be together in Heaven someday. Amen."

i

At four-forty-five the high chime of the alarm cracked his eyelids, and Roman's dreams dissolved into the dark as crisp blood coursed across his irises. His feet, chill and sticky in their night-old socks, swept to the floor as his hand mechanically silenced the clock. Its digital figures contributed a cold pallor to the underside of his forearm and blended, as he drew his hand back, with the white light over the alley, streaking through the bamboo blinds and silvering the faint hairs on the backs of his fingers pressed momentarily to his aching eyes. He'd awoken at that hour, just darker each day, for three weeks now, all through the full fervor of the pilgrimage of Gulf fish into the copulative coastal seas. Each inlet and canal along Lake Pontchartrain seethed with breeding baitfish as well as the schooled and singular predators that harried them ceaselessly.

His mind moved among the fins beneath the darkness, wondering at the flat black eyes, motionless and ever-moved. And his thought surged toward them, forward through the satisfactory sight of his own eyes like red-veined mosaics in the mirror, through the oak-draped avenues and out to the sea in the creaking cradle of the old green Ford; on still through the humid air with the heavy rigs into the green water to wait for the pelagic jaws to strike, all as his flesh struggled from its bedside perch and shuffled through the cold air over the vinyl wood floor. His feet knew the sound spaces and found them on their own, knowing the day depended on escaping the house before his mother could wake and in her aggravation revoke her reluctant approbation of this last morning's fishing. Today was the first of the new school year, the first of four Roman would spend at Ignatius Prep. Beginnings were much with Roman's mother, and it spoke much of her dim trust in his desire that she had approved this final outing at all.

As he urinated in the light of the bathroom's lone yellow bulb, unchanged in ten years, as he washed his face and examined his eyes, absently noting for the third time that week the gold discs scattered about the iris, his mind continued to compose and contemplate the last hour of his leisure, entering at every angle the scene of his hopeful combat, fortifying with all the compounded possibility of a summer's experience this last taste of his time.

He switched off the light, opened the door just enough to admit his frame, thinned with summer's exertions, and crept through the dark den onto the solid tile of the kitchen. His stomach shuddered slightly with the early hour; the sight of yesterday's coffee, left as usual to cool overnight, its oily surface iridescent in the streetlight, further unsettled him. He'd not yet learned to eat before fishing, but he forced himself to take a glass of water as he waited for his father and his brother Michael to appear. Presently they did, and the three took their nine-foot rods from their customary places in the corner of the foyer and stepped into the warm, colloidal darkness of the August morning. For a week now the wind had come calmly and steadily from the West, bringing with it fresher, dirtier water and dulling the spirits of the local fishermen. Roman looked anxiously to the top of the maple in front of the house. It stood still, and his fear abated slightly, though here the wind was always calmer than beyond the levee.

Stooping to a pleasant point of tension in his hamstrings, Roman lifted a twenty-quart blue ice chest from the bed of pine needles beside the front steps. Cool with condensation, it stuck to his purple t-shirt, chilling his belly as he plodded to the green truck. Yesterday's porgies sloshed about inside, the icy slush thickened with their own slime and with the bright scales dulled and loosened in death.

Customarily taciturn and more so with fatigue and anticipation, the three drove in silence to the lake, out beyond the levee and past the mouth of the 17th Street Canal. They needed no bait that day, though the porgies—as the menhaden were then commonly called—schooled in such profusion at the mouth of the canal that a bare hook jerked through the balled-up school would inevitably pierce one of their broad sides, sending the oily fish slicing wildly through the brackish water. There was at that time a bridge across the canal's mouth. Restaurants, bars, parks lined its banks, and couples and small families in droves strolled there on summer evenings, pausing often in the city's climatic indolence to gaze toward the setting Sun and the much greater bridge, the

Causeway. It was a scene popular with painters, and it hung in watercolor counterfeit in many homes. Within three days the bridge would be destroyed, its fragments dragged to the seafloor as well perhaps as into the surrounding neighborhoods. It would not be rebuilt, and those latter-born who saw its image scattered in the homes of relatives and friends would wonder at the irretrievable scene.

In the end of his youth Roman would return often to the place of the bridge, empty but for the broken scores of pilings relieved of the weight of the restaurants they had borne. He came most often then in the evening, but in his mind the bridge remained, transmogrified by yellow streetlights streaming slowly through the night's last hours. The air hung as thick and tangy as the limp nets strung out on the shrimp boats moored along the road, unable in that season ever quite to dry. The porgies popped relentlessly at the surface as though the water had risen to a slight boil. And below them, source of all anxiety, swam the eternal mouths: jacks, sharks, catfish, and the great gars who sometimes ran afoul of the fishermen. Now and then one of their toothy heads, hacked off gratis by some unceremonious Yat, rolled up grinning in the yellow light. Roman had never swum in Lake Pontchartrain.

As our story began, though, possessed as they were of the day's bait, the three Morans drove straight to the Point, a cul-de-sac seawall jutting into Lake Pontchartrain just across the harbor from the Yacht Club. The Point, more than any other place Roman had known, served as salon to the odd congeries of men who in their eccentricity could not have walked down most streets in America unnoticed but who even in large groups went without comment in New Orleans. The only two there thus far were Calvin and Gerry, suitable types of the retired and unemployed men there all those August dawns.

Gerry stood out by virtue of his missing leg and his vocabulary, which clung through fishing's vicissitudes to one word as the octopus clings to coral in a storm. He employed it with such Platonic insistence that Roman had dubbed him the "effin'" king. He was always there early, he was ever there late, and he never moved from his seat on the tailgate of his white pickup. More than once Roman, eyeing askance the round back slowly soaking in sweat as the morning rose, had winced in solidarity with the broad buttocks squashed ceaselessly against the polyurethane liner.

Calvin, it seemed, was always at the Point, and, in point of fact, he had made it his home. He slept in the bed of his white pickup, though where he slept, given the tarps, gasoline cans, odd fishing implements, and magazines which formed his treasure, remained a mystery, as did the question of how he slept, given the regular disturbances occasioned by the violent young men or couples who came there past midnight. He only ever wore a pair of white shorts cut off high on his thighs. They had once been blue jeans. His bare feet—whatever he had inherited or lost by blood, a fantastic Franciscan patrimony had devolved to him down the centuries—shone white against the asphalt and the glittering bits of bottles broken in the night. He never fished himself but seemed simply to appreciate the sea and to gain a satisfaction from the fact that however poor his life might be, there were men--men he met and lived among--who caught fish every day. Today as the Morans pulled up and backed into their customary position, he saluted them, brandishing a twelve-foot length of PVC to which he'd duct-taped a newly sharpened gaff.

"Hey fellas, y'all hook one, just hollah and I'll hawl 'im up. I'mma try to sell 'em in the Quawda today."

"I didn't know people ate 'em," Roman's father answered.

"Aw, yeah, I got a recipe I tell people. Ya cut the meat in strips and lay 'em out on tin foil, ya know? and then ya layer 'em up in buttah an' gahlic and onion and pawsley and whatevah ya want. Then ya bake it for twenty minutes, ya take it out, ya let it cool, and then ya throw the fish away an' eat the foil."

"Hey, shut ya ----- mouth, Cal, feel like I'm chewing ------ foil now!" Mornings agreed badly with the effin king.

"Whatcha gonna do this weekend, Calvin?" Roman's father continued, his eyes drawing back from Gerry in slow defense.

"Ahhh, people keep talkin'. Figure I'mma just ride it out right here. Least if I die there ain't nothin to worry about." Such is the philosophy propounded among many New Orleanians, Stoic with a pre-Socratic elementalism, connected perhaps in some way with its endless collusions of sea and cloud.

As Calvin returned dutifully to his truck, a great creaking of shocks arose along Breakwater Drive, succeeded by a large van, once red, its dull yellow lights dissipating in the darkness. At the first creak Roman had seen the van's driver in memory--shock of grey-brown hair oblivious to gravity, bright blue eyes lined in omnipresent red, one chapped hand lazing on the wheel, the other carefully, rhythmically conducting a Bud Light between a cupholder sticky with dip spit and an ample mustache, duly stained. This Eyckian apparition nosed his vessel into place alongside the Morans, shut off the engine (here Roman heard the water again as for the first time), and sank for a moment into the worn cloth seat, apparently contemplating the dark expanse before him. Presently he stepped down and crowed the day's unofficial commencement.

"Good moornin'------- -----------!"

"Bout -------' time, Billy" Gerry thundered. "My stump's burning like a mutha-------. Been here a God damn hour already."

15

"Not my fault ya got yaself sliced up, ya fat s.o.b." Turning to Roman and Michael, the red face had reddened and curbed its tongue.

"Just gimme a beer, ya dumb drunk ----."

"Whatever I gotta do to shut that mouth, Mr. G."

Billy, an old friend of Roman's father and himself childless, had long since undertaken a nepotistic defense of Roman and Michael's innocence. He harbored a deep faith in the efficacy of fishing as a cure for all social ill, and though it had done him little good as far as the world was concerned, it was a faith he determined to pass on unsullied where he could. For his part, the effect of Gerry's tongue had long since passed in Roman's mind from tragic to comic and on into wonder at his words' vast vacuity, each curse burning and collapsing and clinging to the thought racing on in rage.

"Hey, Jackie, how ya doin? I thought the boys had school today," said Billy, turning to Roman's father.

"Pretty good, pretty good. Yep, Rome starts today."

"Nah! Hey Rome, grab yaself a beer, alright, bud? Don't let it get to ya."

Roman laughed and, unsure of how else to respond, turned and stooped to the ice chest, selected a pogey, pressed the large kahle hook through the latter third of the meaty back, raised his rod over his shoulder and with a light crow hop sent his offering sailing high along the pre-dawn to settle in silent interrogation of the opaque sea.

Around him the men blended their cacophonous measures with the creaking speech of the seabirds, but Roman's mind, withdrawing, kept up a desperate Prime. There remained an element of superstition in his faith, a lingering doubt that all would be well if he should fail to perform the precise offices the cosmos demanded at any given moment, a suspicion that the old men, muttering, 'must not be holdin' my mouth right,' were onto something.

It was most often in the dawn that the best of the day came, and the sea responded quickly as ever that morning. The tip of Michael's rod twitched timidly and then bobbed to an angle of thirty degrees or so as the loose drag clicked pensively. All suggested a Gafftop, a large catfish, particularly slimy, hateful to most fishermen and adored by others for its alleged delicacy. In a minute or so the six-pound fish lay coughing and rolling in the light wrack gathered at the sea-wall's base.

The sight elicited a string of dark Gerardian pronouncements.

"We sure as ---- done for the day now. Slimy ----------a gonna tell all his buddies where the porgies at. And ya know the wawda's ---- when they start biting."

"God damn, Gerry, couldja let ten minutes go by?"

Roman, amused as usual by Billy's gallantry, would normally have disregarded Gerry's prognostications. He had found that New Orleanians, despite their love of amusement and due perhaps in part to native indolence, harbored a deep cynicism concerning life's daily operations. As this would be the last day before operations shifted into another mode, though, Roman felt the cynicism taking hold of him as well.

Light burst then from the sea, red crescent dripping from the waves, flaring in the clouds and setting the white scar of Gerry's stump to flame. In the West the sky unveiled a spectroscopic study in the shades of blue and green, and the gulls leapt from the gentle crests, laughing as they climbed and keeping keen eyes out for their fellows crashing into schools of shrimp or finger mullet. Occasionally one flashed across the Sun, blackening in an instantaneous eclipse to burst again, transfigured, into the dawn.

As though to hail the day three rods bowed to ninety degrees and three reels squealed as three Jack Crevalles, mouths full, swam to sea. Roman grabbed his rod and counted to ten as conscientiously as he could, then tightened the drag and set the hook hard, stepping, almost leaping, back for extra weight. The reels held three hundred yards of light monofilament. One hundred had gone in the take, and now at the sting of the hook the fish almost instantly stripped another hundred, raising the pitch of the reel's whine to pitiful heights. With fifty yards to go the fish slowed and, just as the stripped spool became painfully visible, stopped.

There are two anxious moments in fighting such fish and the first and longest of them was now past and the age-long war had begun. The Jack turned its deep side perpendicular to the line and began to run back and forth in long switchback arcs so that for a dizzying moment Roman pictured the slow progress of a bus back and forth at pained angles up a mountain. Then once more the fish was all.

He gained for some time, and then the fish ran again, but the hook and the leader held firm, and there was little else to fear in the second run. The Sun was higher now and the boy felt the sweat bead in the pores of his back and trickle to the waistline of his khaki shorts. A fly, flaring in the rising light, bounced along his hands and forearms.

Behind him Roman heard a quiet engine followed by a slow, punctual step along the asphalt. In his ear began a calm stream of encouragement in deep, melodious tones. "Let him go, let him go," it advised when the fish ran, or simply, when it turned, "Now, my boy, now."

Haltingly he gained, and the angle of the Jack's arc grew tighter and tighter until at last, some thirty yards out, the fish began to rise unwillingly to the surface. Several times it touched the green surface and set it boiling at each ragged thrash of its sickle-shaped tail.

Here again, as sight fed imagination and the fish grew slowly greater, anxiety welled in Roman's belly, the thought rising again, again, that here, after half an hour's work, all might still be lost.

But he made no mistakes, and the tackle held, and at last the fish, stiff with effort, gasped in the water below, now bright green with the rising South wind. Calvin leaned over the low concrete wall and with a crisp movement jerked the ungainly gaff into the Jack's silver side, out of which spilled a thin red stream as the fish rose from the gentle waves, its yellow tail feeling feebly at the air as it began in leaving the sea to die.

Now as the fish came over the low wall the voice rang out in generous triumph: "Yes, my boy!" Turning, Roman looked into a dark brown face, smiled at a thin white mustache that seemed to float above radiant teeth. Mr. Brady, a retiree of Jamaican extraction perennially dressed in linen shorts and floral shirts, who built his own rods and caught more fish than any of the other Point regulars, had always seemed to Roman to be the gentlest of the men he'd met that summer. He had long awaited the old man's congratulations and he accepted them now with ecstatic silence.

The fish rested a moment in the cigarette butts and bits of glass on the ground. One of its pectoral fins was cut short, whether by some peril or defect, and its large eye lay still, lacking any register of fate. The boy seized it at the base of the tail and hoisted it for pictures, but as he did so the thirty-five-pound bulk slipped slightly, and the hard, sharp fin cut him at the base of his thumb.

After smiling painfully through the weight, he carried the fish to Calvin's truck, where the alban ascetic lashed it to the driver's side of the bed. It hung there alongside four of its fellows, neither the largest nor the smallest, the saffron, cerulean, and silver glowing still against the white paint while the traces of the sea shone on the smooth scales and the rich red blood ran a bit longer.

"Thanks, brotha," said Calvin as he offered the boy an American Spirit from a yellow box, his solitary, inexplicable luxury. The boy took it, not to smoke, for his mother's warnings rang forever in his ears and would circumscribe his field of action for many years still, perhaps as many as remained. A bit of blood from his thumb caught the white paper as he placed it tenderly in the pocket of his shorts, damp with sweat and the slime of the fish.

The Morans, suddenly aware of the sun, haphazardly tossed their gear into the bed of the truck and drove off to prepare for school. The regulars remained there some hours longer, for it was the best day of fishing that season and they landed twenty-seven Jacks among them as well as four bull sharks and one gar which stretched to seven feet and which Billy, a former K-9 officer who considered himself still a serviceman of some sort (indeed, the moniker Billy derived from his delight in the truncheon), dispatched with a 9mm pistol he kept in his glove compartment. The last man to remain was the undertaker (the Morans knew him only by his profession), who talked little and caught more fish than anyone else aside from Brady and who had always finished at least a six pack before he went home. He sat in his foldout chair in the Sun beside his black truck, never sweating despite the heat, the skin of his face growing darker and darker around his black sunglasses. Every twenty minutes or so he hooked another Jack, forced it to the seawall, and then cast another pogey far, far out into the waves, mechanically and lovingly hauling life from the water.

The three wound back along Breakwater Drive toward town, the green truck's shot shocks creaking at each crease in the pavement. As they passed the stilted condos and restaurants, Roman observed a strange undulant stream just above the water to his right. He could not have said whether it was some coordinate insect flight or a compressed defilation of air patterned on the motion of the waves. He thought of pointing out the apparition but decided to keep it for himself, and he continued to think of it when finally they parted from the sea once again at the mouth of the 17th Street Canal. It was at a point less than a mile inland that the wall of that canal would break within a week, spilling millions of porgies as well, perhaps, as some jacks and sharks and gars into the quiet, shady neighborhood the Moran family had called home for fifty years. They would swim in at broken windows and rest, perhaps, in the shelter of submerged bedrooms, and their brackish bones would disintegrate in the autumn ahead, consubstantial with the great stench that would above all form the bed of memory for all who returned.

ii

As her sons and husband sped for home, Eloise Moran gathered testimony from each passing moment in witness to the justice of her anxiety. Each tick of the German clocks scattered around the living room confirmed her. Each pundit's proclamation, pouring in heated profusion from the kitchen radio, renewed her resolve to communicate the nervous state which rose so readily to the places of honor in her mind.

Her ears caught the creak of the old Ford from two blocks. She opened the front door as Roman disembarked, caught the dull sheen of scales on his shirt as he shot through the green shade of the garden.

"Mom, we got one!"

"I can smell," her lips curled upward at the corners as her nose wrinkled. "Hurry up, come on, come on, fifteen minutes!"

"Don't worry, I'll be ready!"

He tripped into the shower, cold water stinging his reddened skin as it warmed. Briefs, socks, sleeves grasped at his wet skin, sodden cereal burst between his teeth as his mother paced, quicker, quicker, forward more upon her toes, casting each time as she passed an unspoken reproach which bawled unceasingly in his ears. First days with her were sacred. And where more sacred than Ignatius Prep, alma mater to her father and brothers and cousins and nephews and surely her own, too, could her father have made her four years a male. Like hummingbirds her senses buzzed from Roman's unbrushed hair to his pungent hands and on to pierce his cut thumb.

Despite, perhaps in virtue of her anxious temper, Roman's mother was deeply, not to say aggressively, pious; indeed, she had nearly joined a convent, and the prayerful joy which had led her there played ever against a violent critical tendency, a compulsion to reprove all fault, physical, mental, or spiritual. From her Roman had inherited a Pelagian ghost. They were, of the four members of their family, most alike, and thus most often at odds.

A cuckoo chimed the quarter hour across the swell of August light in the living room, and time itself concluded its crisis, ushering Roman once more through the door to his mother's promise of prayer through a toothy, thin-lipped smile born of remembered smells of fresh pencils and the feel of clean paper in new notebooks.

The air had grown grossly humid, and Roman, sweating, sat forward in the front seat of the truck as the cold, compressed air flowed around him. He and his father, worn with hard fishing and sleep forgone, sat silent through the short drive to school down the oak-lined portions of Canal and the sprawling planes of treeless cemeteries where the stone angels leaned in smiling or stern adoration over the straight streets. The feeling between them was warm as always, though, and brightened by the morning's success. Jack turned off of Canal down a lane of Creole homes, fuchsia, azure, lilac, and pulled up before the school's black iron gate.

"Go get 'em today, Rome. I'm proud of you."

"Thanks, Dad," and Roman slid from the front seat and waited as his father pulled away once more toward Canal Street. Already he'd begun again to sweat.

iii

From the heart of New Orleans rises a ponderous building of brown brick, its upper stories baking above the green heads of the oaks and gazing off across the budding canopy of the rain trees toward downtown in one direction and Lake Pontchartrain in the other. Seen from above it resembles a large U, its flat hook centered on two majestic wooden doors above which a marble Virgin gazes out over the restless palm-lined avenue; its two arms reach unequally to embrace—or perhaps repulse—the crime-ridden and increasingly fashionable neighborhood in which it sits.

Ignatius Preparatory School has stood in this place for nearly a century, a bastion of learning in a part of the city crumbling quietly through time's common decadence. For all the neighborhood's decline, though, it has remained emblematic of the life of the city, a place where black and white mingle with relative ease, where every house has its porch, each porch its evening watchers speaking freely to the passersby.

The school's shorter, older wing, beside which Roman now stood, runs along Banks Street, where the condensed exhaust of a hundred window units rains through the oak-muted space in rhythmic drops of slowly swollen light to shatter with distinction on the palmettos below.

Up and down the school's long, lofty corridors thundered thousands of young men in khaki uniforms, by-products of the military curriculum adopted in the days between the wars. Indeed, the whole place, much to the sarcastic laughter of its students, evinced an air of the institution. Chain link spanned the first floor windows, and the desks and bulletin boards bore a half-century's abuses at the hands of the inmates who at various periods had risen to run the asylum: dire threats against disciplinarians, surnames and graduation years, absurd sexual declarations to celebrities or, less Olympian, the infrequent female teachers, and, in incomprehensible profusion, penises, rendered across the gamut of idea and energy according to the artists' nascent Academic or Lycean persuasions.

To the visiting eye the erotica stood out less than the trophies and photographs, a seemingly limitless record of victory or its proximate. A century of competitive eyes, photographed at first in stolid black and white and slowly smiling into color, gazed down on the khaki masses, and trophies glinted dully in the white fluorescent lighting. There were trophies in display cases, trophies in cabinets, trophies in desks and on floors and in closets, forever to remind and to reproach.

Artistic decoration, by contrast, was spare but striking: white sculptures of the Virgin, Ignatius, and Xavier; a smattering of prints by Dali and Michelangelo and Goya in the rooms of the more aesthetically-minded teachers, and a pair of original paintings by a student in the class of '28, one of the school seal and the other of St. Francis Xavier on-board ship, gazing at the shore of Japan. This latter was a rare wonder of artistic and spiritual insight, the colors vibrant, almost garish, and the perspective, horizontal to the wave-tipped ship's window, disorienting.

Each arm of the school housed a chapel. The larger, used for school-wide Masses, was simple, Romanesque, with one stained glass window above the altar, a Sacred Heart reminiscent of El Greco ringed with sacramental images in porphyry and sapphire. The pews were long and close-set with the swollen student body, of a pale wood carved here and there with names but luckily, or perhaps by force of proxim deity, spared the phallic blemish.

The other chapel--the small chapel as it was commo called--though in slight disrepair at the time, its red carpe tattered and thin, the gold filigree dull, remained a favorite with visitors and the more spiritual of the students. Stained glass Saints and Stations ringed the transept and altar, and a great glass dome housed the descending Holy Spirit in thin shards shaped and shaded like leaves in decay's eternal bloom. A score of students celebrated Mass there each morning, kneeling as the stained light roved over them.

Roman entered this building ninety minutes after landing his Jack, and he spent one day there before its state altered dramatically, though not in the particulars related above.

Wading through the sea of shouting uniforms in the oak-lined courtyard, catching scents of body spray and sweat and the peculiar stench of boys who've not yet recognized their bloom, Roman at length found Francis Higgins, a vague relative of the man whose ships saw the Allies onto Normandy's beaches and Roman's best friend since infancy. Francis's pale skin seemed more so today, and his eyes, which typically straddled an ill-defined border between blue and green, were decidedly blue. He had evidently tried to order his hair, which grew in coarse black waves across his skull, to no avail.

"So it begins."

"Four more years," Roman said. Glancing about, he noticed a group of seniors evidently engaged in a chocolate milk drinking contest. A year later he would have laughed.

"Hell, our dads made it."

"Yeah."

A bell sounded, and the rings of students broke, swelled against each other, and coalesced once more in rows according to homeroom for morning assembly. Roman stood

ιround him exchanged excited greetings
unts of the summer. Most of them had
before. He, however, knew no one in his
a few students in any of his classes, and
·browed silence.

ιιcy man, are you depressed or something?" asked a soft, high-pitched voice to Roman's left. He turned, amused as much as self-conscious, and looked down into a round, pale face pocked with rash which ran down the boy's neck, vanished beneath his collar, and spread along his white, hairless arms. Roman gazed in silence on this smiling apparition.

"You just look kinda depressed. It's awesome here!"

"Not again."

"Really, Delery?"

"Shut the hell up, Del, this place sucks!" snapped several voices like mouse traps.

The bell tolled again, and Fr. Peregrine Muller, president, ascended the podium. Roman had met him regularly at Mass at the Jesuit parish downtown as well as in his own home, where his mother maintained an irregular salon. Over the sudden silence came a brief prayer and his salutatory address:

"None of you who know me will be surprised at what I have to say this morning. We have maintained a tradition of excellence here for many years now, and I expect we will continue that tradition this year. We must take care, though, not to allow that tradition to blind us to our own weaknesses or to allow us to grow complacent. Along with our excellence we have developed a reputation in this community for arrogance, for believing that we are somehow elite. To enter the ranks of the human elite is something none of us are ever likely to experience. You'll hear people talk about our 'elite' baseball program, for instance, a program that in sixty years and thousands of players has produced just three who made careers of baseball and only one household name.

"Part of our alleged elitism arises from a lie we tell ourselves with devilish regularity. How often do we hear it said that you can be whatever you want to be as long as you work hard enough? That's a lie! You may want more than anyone else who's ever lived to be a professional basketball player or musician or writer. But no amount of desire, no amount of hard work, without the aid of grace, suffices for us.

"Fortunately, however, we believe that God does not ask us to be elite, at least not elite in the scheme of human achievement. He has a plan for each one of us, a plan whereby he intends for us to join him one day in the unity of the Saints. This unity, gentlemen, is the only elite circle to which we should aspire, for it is the only one which transcends the narrow cinctures of human excellence. It is a gift, one which we can receive best by performing the work God has laid out for us each day for His greater glory. Let us be about that work today."

The light in the courtyard had brightened and Roman felt the sweat roll down his spine again.

A boy with caramel-colored skin and a short shock of curly black hair ascended the podium then to loud acclamation from the senior homerooms ringing the podium. He read the announcements for the day, here pausing dramatically, now eyeing his audience with conspiratorial mirth. The crowd obliged him at each juncture. Roman noticed that even many of the teachers were laughing, though most of them, moments prior, had looked as grim as he felt.

Another bell rang, and Roman, trying to maintain his motive power in the crowd which suddenly resolved into six or seven currents, made his way to the third floor and into his Geometry classroom just before the bell rang. He thought through the morning of his fish as he passed, dazed, through lectures on postulates and cellular structure and a bewildering introduction to macrons and penults. Everywhere he found himself surrounded by circles of students, rings of acquaintance strengthening their members against the new beginning's gloom. He longed in spite of his reticence to become part of one of these cadres.

He and Francis met again at the door of the Sacred Scripture class, an old room on the third floor occupied by an even older man who bustled about with an energy suggestive of response to the yawning grave ahead. Andrew Ruggieri's appearance, which can't have been a comfort to himself each morning, looming pale in the mirror as some deep sea fish, was enough to thoroughly disturb any fourteen-year-old. He was quite tall, though his thick, drooping shape caused him to appear rather shorter. Hair bristled almost imperceptibly from his spotted scalp; his mouth hung slightly open and his lip shone with a barely dammed stream of drool. Slowly though, the smile lines about his mouth and eyes, which were at once very dark and exceedingly luminous, grew more apparent.

The bell rang, but the boys, half the day behind and lunch ahead, remained huddled in loose groups, chattering about their summers and groaning under the already unconscionable weight of homework.

"Sit down, ya little -----!"

Twittering, the boys rushed to their seats. From reminiscent uncles and the uproarious schoolyard, most of them had heard so much of the man before them that his words now worked a comic consummation. Roman and Francis exchanged wide-eyed stares. Again the brief bolt of nothing. At their previous school the older students had whispered curses with a frequency and facility which would have scandalized at least most of their parents, but any such obscenity on the lips of teachers should have been met . swift and terrible discipline.

"Get this out," Ruggi (he had been known thus by generations of students) said, holding up a Bible.

When the Book appeared on twenty-five desks, Ruggi dropped his to the floor. A thud succeeded the ripple of pages. In the silence the boys stared; the old man stared back, almost smiling.

"This is a book, a story in most ways like any other. It does not possess magical properties. It doesn't teach you any spells. Neither does Christ. His ways are mysterious, but they are rational, and we can begin to understand them by intense study.

"Now tell me something—how long did it take God to create the world?"

Several voices murmured, "Seven days."

"Come on, come on, call it out. Six, in fact, and one for rest. So what's a day?"

A pause. "Twenty-four hours?"

"Sure, sure, but where do we get that?"

"Earth's rotation."

"How do we know earth rotates?"

"The Sun."

"Exactly." Pause. "When did God create the Sun?" He smiled.

A silence followed, broken only by the stealthy flicking of thin pages.

"Not until the fourth day?" one boy volunteered hesitantly.

"Precisely. Now what does that tell us?"

Another pause followed, and then Francis said, as one noticing a common beauty, "That the days in Genesis aren't twenty-four-hour days."

"Bingo. See how much we take for granted? Starting right now I want you to question everything. If you learn nothing arn that. People see the word day and assume

once you assume that, you have to say the

s were either liars or idiots. They're neither.

ts, poets, people in love with what they know, reaching out and breaking through the hard rind of everyday experience to see the reality beyond. Questioning everything."

And so on in Socratic examination of Genesis One. Roman's mother had read Scripture to him and had always encouraged him to read it himself, but he had never experienced it as an object to be studied. Where through the morning his mind had cast about it now reveled in a weightless depth, though Ruggieri himself left him in some way uneasy. He was haunted by the image of his mother seated at the back of the room, her face now quizzical, now flushed, shaking slowly, tilted to the left as though by some heretic freight. He could not have placed the weight precisely, though perhaps it was simply that he had entered a realm in which the rules of discernment remained yet hidden.

Nevertheless, he enjoyed himself to the point that he forgot the hunger which had begun to gnaw the previous period. At length the bell rang once again, and Roman and Francis returned to the courtyard, now sweltering in the August noon, for lunch.

As they pressed through the seething and ravenous crowd, down a dim green flight of stairs, Roman noticed Francis glancing up at him over his shoulder, smiling faintly as if through a Pythian exhalation. He said nothing, however, until they'd sat in the thin shade of a young oak, where he offered typically trenchant comment on the morning's proceedings.

Roman, sullen in the noontime sun, sat in silence through most of lunch, occasionally offering a simple yes or no or laugh as the basic patterns of their friendship required. His mind shrank more and more from the memory of Scripture. He was, by nature, curious, but he limited his inquisitions to the natural. On matters of authority, he had learned, both from his mother's adoration of the powerful and his father's swift and stern tongue, that questions bred hardship.

Through the afternoon classes Roman felt the day's loneliness redouble. It was Friday, in keeping with a tradition which held that a week of one day worked wonders for morale. Roman, however, had always met the first Friday of the school year in anxiety, with its false sense of an ending at the outset of an endless series of exercises so often vain, delivered by a series of teachers whose consuming languor evanesced irregularly into rage.

A faint stir rose through the rest of the students, though, as rumor of the coming storm grew more menacing, and in this stir lived a fraternity of sensibility in which Roman could participate, a ring binding all New Orleans. Storm could mean a week off of school, a spontaneous vacation, a swell of cooler air. For Roman hurricane days recalled the awe of waves breaking from the swollen lake along the levee and the levity of the gale. They meant wading ankle deep in cool floodwater, even kayaking down familiar streets. They called for water and candlelight. In those days New Orleanians looked to the portents of disaster in the way Neapolitan children may once have gazed wistfully at the grumbling wisps about Vesuvius' head.

Just before three o'clock a voice came over the intercom: "Good afternoon. Due to the impending storm the archdiocese has called for the closure of all schools Monday and Tuesday of next week. Thank you." Jubilation reigned. And Roman rioted with his fellows in the confidence of comedy.

iv

At last the day's final bell rang, and the sea of khaki ebbed and dispersed, mostly into cars queued in the courtyard or down the streets along the school. Roman walked alone up Solomon Street to Canal. Three o'clock was too early for either of his parents to pick him up, and so they had decided that the streetcar and the bus would serve until he could drive. Since his early school years he had taken comfort in public spaces, in buses, grocery stores, shopping centers, in walking among people whose concerns ranged beyond the scope of the scholastic, for though he recognized in an academic sense the need for education he had always found that school sickened his heart, killing his leisure and carrying off his Sundays like so many Sabine women; being among regular people bound with what he conceived as the actual concerns of existence always affirmed his own being at least by reference to some similar future.

He climbed onto the green car and sat about halfway down its length across the aisle from a pretty blonde woman about twenty, a tourist, judging from her camera and her Aryan appearance. He affected a glance past her as the trolley trundled in front of St. Anthony of Padua, its white marble facade bright in the now golden afternoon. Her dark sunglasses flashed as they turned, blank and pitiless, toward him; and she smiled lightly, likely, he thought, in amusement at his uniform, and he flushed as he looked away.

Back at home, sweaty and wracked again by malaise, Roman trod slowly toward his room, his black shoes squeaking on the clean cherry floors. In the dark hallway he met Bandit, the border collie, large for his breed but not yet obese as he would later become. For any other member of the family he would have risen and run to the door, but his relations with Roman had always been more cordial than warm, and his eyes alone followed the boy down the hall as his tail beat a gentle triplet greeting.

Perched on the edge of his bed, Roman relaxed slightly as his gaze rested on a mounted redfish, not particularly large but bound up with perfect memory, and swung slowly over the mural on the facing wall, a swamp scene by the old woman who long before had attempted to teach him to draw. The silence pressed him until he rose, returned to the hall, and called Francis, who said he was doing nothing and to come over and to bring his guitar.

Possibly it was propinquity alone that had cemented the boys' friendship. Their mothers had met via a mothers' social group, and, finding they lived but two blocks apart, despite the utter variance of mien and habit between them, became fast friends as did their sons. Francis's younger brother, Andrew, was the same age as Michael. The four, all in the same school, had spent the better part of the past ten years in each other's company. Often, in the car home, they would ask in conspiratorial tones the awful and wide-eyed question, "Do you want to ask?" A representative would then be chosen to propose Roman and Michael stay till dinner at the Higgins house, and the invariant affirmative meant two more hours together, usually passed at basketball or football or any number of games inherited or invented in the alley and the back yards of the indulgent neighbors.

Five minutes after placing the phone call, Roman turned up the straight stone walk to his friend's door. The house, an aged cottage, originally of red brick, had on some whim been painted a light blue whose shade refused to lodge in Roman's mind. Again now it startled him, and, awaiting admittance, he studied it anew. It eluded him. Wherever his eye sought to light it seemed somehow to vanish into white. Half-frightened, he blinked rapidly. The door opened and now he found himself awash in the *Tannhauser Overture*, its somber radiance mingling with the slight scent of fish and the redolence of fallen magnolia leaves which clattered across the sidewalk in the afternoon's faint breath. Immediately he fell in with the rhythm of the house, the romance of song in its forever lost eternity cycling through the living room, motionless but for Francis's mother curled in a chair at the window, predictably parting the leaves of her modish novel.

Upstairs the boys situated their instruments and amplifiers on the cool, cream-colored carpet and then washed their hands, a precept of Francis's musical apostolate which for Roman had never jelled with the state of his friend's fingers. They were and always had been ugly—rough with birthmarks, damp and clammy even to the eye. None seeing his hands should have guessed at their beauty, for it was born not of nature but in grim obedience to a deep hunger. Roman's mother—and he, too, to a much stricter extent—had a talent for music. She had come home from Mass at some tender age of legend, approached the piano, and without hesitation or exploration played a hymn. Roman had never seen her struggle at the keys, never observed her at a loss as to the melody of a song, even if she had heard it only once twenty years prior. Myth of a Rooseveltian sort surrounded her. Nonetheless her hands, too, were ugly—large, bony, pale, brightly veined. They were hands as of an ancient life lingering in the magic of their act. Yet their knuckled flight elicited awe and even, on occasion, love.

The boys began to play, seated on the floor in customary silence, fingers stiff at first with expectation. Steered by Francis' taste and diligence they had grown adept in a stark brand of neo-classicism. Confidence warmed as their fingers limbered over liquid arpeggios and frantic triplet runs. Occasionally as Roman slurred a phrase Francis, eyes down and head shaking slowly, would mutter, "Come on, come on." There was little art in Roman's playing in those days. By a brutal pride his pick at times surpassed his friend's in speed, but his left hand lacked Francis's legatic grace. Roman, truth be told, could at best be called a dilettante, and not truly in a musical sense, for his delight was in Francis, in being with him and tasting the fruits of his efforts at the strings stirring, ripening, and falling at the silvery vibrations.

After three quarters of an hour they paused. The light, angling through the backyard magnolias, had fallen upon them, and as Francis withdrew to the bathroom Roman stood and strolled around the large room, the backs of his knees cool with sweat. Briefly examining the book shelves, he paused at Francis's desk and looked over the jumble of papers there, greasy and graffitied in Francis's fat and rambling characters. In a corner lay a crumpled page cut from the sports section of the paper; noticing the date, Roman wondered why his friend had saved it, until after a moment he noticed in the bottom right corner a strip club advertisement. A splendid blond stood statuesque along the right margin, her right hand teasing her top back just beyond a nipple to contribute a disproportionate share of Bourbonic enticements. No doubt an editor, rushed or simply inured, had slipped; blood beat in Roman's ears until, closing his eyes and shaking his head, he averted his gaze.

Strewn elsewhere about the desk were bits of what looked like poetry. One page in particular caught his eye:

A storm stole up from the African coast
and stole the dark beauty I measured most,
and while he and she stole time on the town
I stole God's heart and I drowned and I drowned.

Never has weather done more to destroy
since Patroclus lay in the blood below Troy
and the storm stole up from the minstrel's fire
and fire's dark light dreamed love's last desire.

His reading broke off as the toilet flushed and Francis emerged with a contented air.

"Wanna go to the football game tonight?"

"Too hot. Why would they have a game this early in the year?"

"And you say you'll never leave."

"Where would I go?"

According to his then current understanding, Roman's family on his father's side had come to New Orleans from Ireland in 1826, on his mother's from Sicily in 1912. Three members had left the city in the intervening ages, one on mission to China as a Franciscan, two by marriage to Colorado. Departures were thus considered shocking, not to say miraculous, and it was only a Dionysian creativity which could bring them off successfully. Those who had attempted to leave under less artful auspices had all slunk back and set up quiet but prosperous groceries.

"Alright, well, do you want to just spend the night here?"

"Long as I can borrow some stuff."

"Always."

That settled, and the light decayed to evening's reasonable pitch, they decided on a game of basketball. It passed as most of their countless contests had on the cracked drive behind the garage and would have borne no comment but for a curious impasse it left in Roman's memory.

They played to twenty-one points, and as ever when the game had reached its closing skirmishes and the sweat had oiled them everywhere save on their hands, dark with the dust of the alley, an unspoken anger had surged into their play. What in the early stages had been natural contact became at these cruxes sharp and slippery jolts into each other's chests and sides.

Roman led 20-19, and when Francis, breaking too quickly for his flank, slipped, Roman seized the ball and made brutally for the basket. As he rose for the shot Francis leapt with him, and for a moment both touched the ball, struggling tenuously;

finally the leather slipped past Francis's long fingers and rattled awkwardly into the net.

They touched ground and Roman felt a touch of the anger still and a hint of some sickness at the victory. Then Francis's voice, quiet and joyful, enveloped him: "I love you, man." From the edge of his still-clouded vision Roman saw his friend smiling softly at him. Slowly he met his eye. He said nothing, though they both laughed softly, and after a few more haphazard shots they adjourned to the air conditioning. Francis lent Roman two t-shirts, one to dry sweat and another to wear afterward. Their smell, of a stale potpourrian sweetness, remained to Roman a constant reminder throughout the evening.

They made their beds that night on the floor on either side of a nook from which shone the alley's yellow light. It lay heavy on the carpet between them, and through its medium they spoke.

"Have you heard from Amy?"

Francis' breathing deepened slightly, with what sort of memory Roman couldn't have said. "No, not from her. Mary said she was with some guy, though."

"With?"

"With."

Roman felt he had misspoken, and he cast around for some amendment. Presently a thought, beaten back for several months, returned to him, and he felt his belly warming as hesitantly he set forth his secret.

Throughout their youth and with a growing gravity the two had confessed themselves to one another, and in these confessions they had contributed to each other's weight in good and evil. A deep heat surged into their speech and urged them into distant provinces of image.

Now and then Roman thought with slight regret of the scene then playing in his parents' home, of the tinted candlelight and recorded Gregorian chant and a decade of the Rosary. He could not have known that after this night the curtain would descend on that scene forever, and on thousands of scenes that had played regularly in the homes of families secure in decades of scheduled comfort. He could not have known that even as across the yellow light he and Francis stirred each other's blood the feast of the great fish beyond the levee had risen to a savage hysteria.

Near midnight, unsure if Francis slept, Roman drifted into a dream. He sat in a small boat, rolling gently in the mild waves. The light, curiously strong, seemed to strike him from every angle, and as he looked around, unable to find the sun, he saw a bird descending. Soon it took the form of a pelican, hung for a moment suspended as if in choice, and dove. As it shattered its crescent reflection, Roman's eyes seemed to sharpen, and he watched as the water rushed through the short feathers of its face, as the great pouch filled and the long bill snatched a frantic mullet, its eyes rolling in fright.

Then the bird turned and rose toward the light, and as it did the wings spread, and the feathers fell away on the water. The gular membrane broadened and swelled as the bill pressed to the chest. The eyes widened as they moved apart, a nose rose and red lips blossomed, and the yellow feathers of the head billowed into golden hair. The feet deepened, grew slender, and the legs stretched, curved, ripened, as gentle ringlets curled.

Roman warmed at the woman beside him on the sea, now dead-calm. His hand went forth and with an effort passed to a marble-white shoulder to wake her. And though the light was warm her skin at once chilled the tips of his fingers, and he drew back, noticing too now between the breasts a dagger of slender design.

He warmed now again and a sudden voice whispered that the knife was his, that it would draw him out by any means he wished. Slowly, with reverie's weight, he stretched himself toward it, and a sickness came upon him.

Then he felt himself falling, and looking up he found Francis in the shroud of the dim light, gazing down on him and gently pressing his upturned right palm.

II.

INTO SOMETHING RICH AND STRANGE

And then seven, and the dove hovered high above the beaten gold altar that had taken highest prize in Paris, hovered higher than the marble Virgin conceived for Sainte Chappelle and ported to New York in iconoclastic terror now gazing out above the golden onion domes toward the river through the rose acrylic window and the face of her dying Son.

And he stood below her on the altar with the other boy and the bear-like Irish priest who preached so briefly of our imminence, who had plunged him into infant grace and who would be dead before his brother first communed and who had asked him in confidence what is the Eucharist to which he'd said, stuttering 'the bl-body and blood of God' and who now pronounced him worthy of the blood and would tip it to his lips.

And he thought as he looked out on the brushed and perfumed or homeless congregation, the faces he had mostly known from beside or from behind, sitting downtown where the Society's great plantation had bloomed, of the dove so far above which he had watched so many times since earliest memory, gazing up from the wood and iron past the shoulder of his father who seemed so tall, past the chandeliers and the higher and highest stained light at the dove large as an eagle cast in gold and gazing down at the marble with talons poised, and fear seized him that the dove now hovering behind him might descend unseen to pierce his shoulders and rush through the great glass rose and drop him unforgiven in the dark river carrying the continent's sickness to the Gulf where the great fish swam beneath the reaches of the Sun.

i

Mrs. Margaret Moran, Roman's grandmother, had lived in the same house for nearly half a century. A large, squat structure of pale brown brick, it stood on a prominent corner overlooking Canal Boulevard, ringed by tall pines and pecans and a great oak which stretched away from the house over the street to the neutral ground. For her this tree--the most beautiful of all the oaks she had known, according to her appropriate bias--was the home's essential feature.

Flowers—roses, zinnias, pentas, a host of others whose names Roman had so often heard bandied among his aunts—proliferated in the back yard. Birds winged vividly, the cardinals and the blue jays and the little passerine sopranos, drawn by a central stone bath and insect abundance. Squirrels' nests hung clustered in the canopy, where the shadowy tenants raced about in their endless collections of pine cone and pecan, leaping often over the hammock spread in the yard's back corner where the grandchildren lay in a roiling heap of long, thin, pallid limbs.

Around the garden ran a path of rough, square paving-stones, and it had been one of Roman's chief pleasures during holiday gatherings and warm Spring mornings alone with his grandmother to lift the stones in search of insects: muscular earthworms, columns of ants startled in their shallow mines, spiders who scuttled angrily, eyes glittering, into the grass, and never slugs themselves but always the tracks of their passage iridescent in the morning light on the smooth-packed earth. His delights ever frightened him, and he took care to lift the stones only by their bright edges.

The interior of the house, well-lit and ordered, innocent of the rash of disrepair so soon supervenient on the veil of the elder widowed, was split into three levels. Certain elements of its design had so melded with Roman's memory that, long after he had forgotten the features of his own home, they yet remained, fed of the intimacies and observations of the four generations of Morans who at one time or another had lived there: an inexplicable stationary bicycle whirring in the cool, dim den; a grate of balsa opening onto the dark space below the stairs; the stairs themselves, of pale wood worn wan; a pair of small wooden squirrels residing in the mailbox; a clock on the cupboard which chimed the quarter-hours in London tones.

On the morning after entering Ignatius Prep, Roman sat in Grandma Moran's old kitchen for the last time, listening to the clock's final attended measures. His father, finding Roman unusually unhelpful in the work of packing and securing the house, had sent him in to sit with Grandma. So Roman, squirming now and then in Grandma's gaze, sipped a glass of the bitter iced tea his Uncle Joe brewed every day and breathed the smell of the house, redolent of something between oatmeal and cinnamon and old carpet.

Grandma looked at him steadily, unblinkingly, across the mahogany table scarred here and there by the seven children it had fed. "And what did you think of Ignatius, Roman?" She had a way, no less charming for its disconcerting quality, of beginning conversations with the word "and."

"It seems alright so far." He took a long sip of tea. The ice cubes bumped against his teeth in chill indolence.

Here Uncle Joe's white sneakers clumped into the kitchen. In each hand he bore a small wooden train. "Ma, ya think we oughtta take any a' these?"

She raised her head, tilted it just to the right, said, "Well, maybe just put them upstairs, would you?"

"Yeah, alright," he moaned as he heavily withdrew. Uncle Joe, the last of the seven children and Roman's godfather, had emerged from the womb misshapen in the slightest measure, unnoticeable except by vague intuition before a sure sight of his hands, each with only four fingers, shaped rather like big toes and coated in coarse black hair. By this oddity the others disclosed themselves more plainly: a slight disproportion about the face, a tendency toward tears in the large, luminous eyes. These seemed later, in far-off, lonely reflections on that unprecedented delivery, to portend Mr. Moran's passage, the slow decay of form to be completed within two years of Joe's birth.

Brushing his teeth, tying his shoes, writing especially, had all in Joe's boyhood and even into his adolescence thus been great tasks for him; nonetheless, an astute teacher had discovered his extraordinary facility in wood. Toy train sets, vanities, armoires, chests of drawers, cribs, cradles, and bookshelves processed from his shop shrouded in their own lignite musk to the delight of his many nieces, nephews, cousins, and siblings. The trains had formed part of the irreplicable mechanism of many a Moran family gathering, and Roman, too, felt the reluctance of his uncle's retreating tread.

Still Grandma, turning back from Joe's inquiry, smiled at Roman. It was a smile disarming and girlish, as were most of her characteristic postures. She was not at all like the ladies Roman would later come to think typically Southern: blonde, slim, streamlined; never unsmiling in company nor laughing unreservedly; all accomplished cooks with eyes for form and for color expressed most exquisitely in gardens; heiresses in his mind to the heroines of English romance.

Indeed, none of Roman's family fit this description. Most of his aunts, beautiful even into grandmotherhood, spent an untoward amount of time in hysterical laughter, often at crudities. They were different from their mother, perhaps because their father had died so young and none of their husbands had. Yet they bore within them the dignity and courage which for Roman characterized his grandmother as the archetypal Southern woman, unrefined by wealth or wealth's genetics and in her unrefinement possessing and dispensing a grace which only a girl can have, the grace of waves and of plain poetry telling the simple stories which waves whisper darkly to the land.

"I imagine you all are so much smarter than we were," Grandma now said. "We mostly just memorized things; I learned a lot of poetry then."

"I wish we could memorize poetry."

"You do like poetry, don't you, Roman," she said, as if remembering. "I think you got that from me. Your grandfather didn't care too much for poetry. He only knew one poem, in fact." She cleared her throat with a kind of musical grunt and began the lines Roman had heard at least a dozen times in the last two months. Her mind and tongue had grown so habituated to each other that they delivered, without any rehearsal, the same speeches verbatim, and with an unerring precision of inflection, even at intervals of many years.

"Well here it is, spring.
The birds are on the wing.
Well ain't that absurd?
I thought the wings were on the bird."

She paused and looked at him comically: "Pretty bad stuff, huh?"

They laughed together then, her musical chortle rising to a dignified peak and then descending again into her throat. It was a laugh her daughters had inherited and stretched to incontinent proportions and it seemed to Roman utterly artless.

Presently, there irrupted shouts from the next yard: "HEY! JOE! GET DA HELL OUT HEAH!"

Roman had grown used to such outbursts. George Eliot Thomason had on more than one Mardi Gras occasion ridden enthroned *en toilette* through New Orleans' most elegant avenues. A long-time neighbor now decrepit in early middle age, he had taken up in place of Divine Office a series of shouting matches, rich with arcane nuance, with Uncle Joe, who gladly reciprocated. Roman and Grandma turned their attention to the dining room window, upon whose province Uncle Joe, having raced down the steps, now burst, himself shouting: "WHAT?! WHAT?! WHAT DA HELL YA TALKIN BOUT?!"

Roman's father entered the room then, sweating and grim-faced, slightly out of breath. "Would you give me and Grandma a minute, Rome?"

Roman, grateful, stepped lightly from the room and bounced down the three steps into the cool lower level where the air was sweet with laundry detergent and the odors of the flowers wafting indolently through the screen door. He creaked through the screen, tripped down three more steps of concrete, and crossed the lawn to the hammock. After gazing up through the light green leaves of the pecan tree to the bright blue sky feathered with cloud, he allowed his eyes to flutter shut.

He had woken that morning in a heap of blankets and pillows on the floor of Francis's room. In place of the night's dim yellow light there now fell the clear morning, though looking out, stomach sore with his brief sleep, he saw that the lamp still glowed, ineffectual against the sun. He would have slept much longer were it not for Mrs. Higgins' voice, clear and clipped, calling him. He and Francis had stumbled downstairs, blinking and tousle-haired, to meet Roman's father, who apologized for coming so early but said they had to go home and pack.

There are certain days when the psyche, touched perhaps by its animal sensitivity, manages in the moment to measure the moment's import. Certain days whisper the joy of their greatness to the mind in its first waking. Other days portend intransigent tragedy. This was one of the latter for Roman. He could not have said how, for in its approach there was little to distinguish this storm from those others which had called for evacuation, but he sensed an ending.

Roman and Francis, who had not to this point in their lives passed more than a week without each other's company, parted then, not to see each other for another forty days. They had discussed the storm the night before, Roman's unconcern disturbed only slightly by Francis's saying his family would not evacuate ("We always do and nothing ever happens.") Something at last would happen; indeed, for many who did not evacuate, the last would happen.

Roman and his father walked home, mostly in the shade of trees fated to fall within the week. They walked in silence wrought with unwonted tension. As they approached their house, he saw a large dent, almost a gash, in the passenger door of his father's truck.

"What happened?"

His father looked up from the ground. "Bumped a fire hydrant on my way out of the gas station." Roman's father, despite his standing as an upholder of the law, took a liberal view of traffic regulations; nonetheless, he was a driver of extraordinary grace and precision, and Roman had known him to make a mistake behind the wheel only once, and then in flight to the hospital.

Entering by the white front door, Roman saw the foyer lined with suitcases and six stacks of thick photo albums. Jack noticed them, stopped, called to his wife. She emerged from the home's rear hallway, her sneakers sharp against the wood floor.

"El, we can't take all these."

"I can't leave them."

Evacuation has revealed to most New Orleanians their idols. For Roman it was an illustrated copy of *Swiss Family Robinson* which had belonged to his grandfather. For Francis it was his Les Paul. For Eloise Moran it was her photo albums. Her family's home had flooded in her teenage years, destroying all photographic record of her infancy. She had determined to save the boys their history.

Jack gazed at the stacks for a moment, then shook his head and said, "They go in last." Then he hurried off to pack his own small bag and secure the house and the garden shed for departure.

An hour later they drove away: two cars, four people, one border collie, a guitar, two computers, forty-five books, seven suitcases, and thirty-seven photo albums, not including Grandma and Uncle Joe and their various treasures. For four weeks they could not return, and almost all not in the cars was lost.

ii

Evacuation *en masse* would not begin for twenty-four more hours, and the traffic flowed from the city as steadily as on any Saturday, past the spillway where the nests of bald eagles knotted the upper reaches of the cypresses and into the swamp and wet meadowlands of South Central Louisiana.

After two hours the Morans reached St. Francisville, a hamlet near Baton Rouge, and checked into a hotel recommended by Francis's mother, whose own mother had been born nearby and who yet nurtured a lonely love of its rolling oak forests and alluvial farms.

The hotel was a small, spotless two-story building, blue with white trim. Its broad, neighborly balconies looked off across golf courses to a vast pine wood. Nestled in the course were small brown ponds, and behind the hotel, through thickets of bamboo, ran a wide, slow creek. It was the scene of their first endurance. For Roman and Michael it was one of exultant beauty; for their mother it became a torment.

Before long cars began to fill the parking lot, cars packed in fashion similar to theirs. Cramped and nervous dogs sprang from dandered seats, children chased each other on the manicured lawns, and parents, mostly laughing, excited as their children, mingled over coolers of beer. It was the social stage necessary to every evacuation, a time when the sweat had dried and the dread anticipation of the crucial moments remained distant. By evening some thirty families had gathered, met, established whatever connections existed among them. One of the men worked in Jack's office. Four of them were members of the Yacht Club. Six belonged to St. Dominic's Parish. None were worried. They cooked massive vats of jambalaya and gumbo in the parking lot and by dint of bowl, spoon, and bottle soon passed the evening. The voices of seven different newscasters, broadcast in anxious tones, strove to remind the assemblage of the danger ahead. None were disturbed. No memory served to disturb them.

Slowly and by comforting degrees the sky darkened and the wind mounted in the high pines all around. The families began to disperse to their suites, though some of the men, insomniac by some animal instinct, waited up through the night, slowly sipping, listening to the news in their cars. By dark the crests of the pines had begun to swing through slow and varying arcs, creaking in climbing pitch.

The air grew close within the Morans' suite. Grandma looked sedately around, now and then by some pleasant inquiry fanning the faltering conversation. Uncle Joe, seated on the floor, back to the base of a couch, passed a smiling hour playing with the dog, who licked him endlessly, unused to such a warm reception. Eloise paced, inspecting the suite on points of cleanliness inscrutable to anyone else and glancing angrily now and then toward Uncle Joe. Roman sat on the floor with Michael, who showed him the contents of an old fly fishing vest, now amply stocked with three knives, two scissors, four flashlights, twelve batteries, a roll of duct tape, fifty feet of paracord, a compass, and six bullets. Roman raised an eyebrow at this last, surreptitious revelation.

Michael, prepared for any such infidel reaction, said, "You're gonna be the last one I save if something goes wrong."

"If something goes wrong I respectfully request to be the last person you try to save."

"Eloise, thank you so much for letting us stay with you," Grandma said suddenly, her chin held high and at a slight angle, her jaw trembling with the effort of maintaining her smile.

"Oh..." Eloise said in a tremulous, high-pitched sigh, her habitual response to pleasantries she could not return. She glanced once again toward Bandit and Uncle Joe, chortling happily as he pet the thick black coat. Roman noticed her glance now and, wondering what had fixed her distress, followed it. A dull red rash of some kind had spread around Uncle Joe's ankles and calves. He felt something of his mother's anxiety then: Bandit had licked the rash; who knew what else he might lick. She called to him, "Roman, would you come here a minute?" She turned toward the bedroom, beckoning forcefully, once she'd gained the cover of the short hallway, for him to follow.

"Why didn't you say anything about Uncle Joe's rash?" she began in a harsh, cracking whisper.

"How was I supposed to know about it?"

"It's your dog and your godfather out there."

Similar in sensibility as he was to his mother, Roman could summon no safe response. So, with perhaps equal danger, he simply walked out of the room, through the living area and out onto the balcony, where a light rain now fell in silence through the cooler air. He sneezed and a voice to his right said, "God bless you." Turning, he saw an old man, illuminated faintly by the streetlight in the parking lot.

"Do you know why they say, 'God bless you'?" he said.

"I heard somebody say one time it's 'cause your soul comes out of your body for a second."

"No, no, no, it's 'cause the devil's trying to make room to get inside."

"Isn't it the same thing?" Roman asked.

"It's completely different." And the old man lit a cigarette and walked away down the long balcony. Roman never saw him again. His father approached him from the opposite direction, returning from listening to the radio in his car. His face was slack with wear and in the shadowy streetlight it seemed old. With a dim glance he passed Roman into the living room. The temperature seemed to have risen. His mother had not reemerged from the bedroom.

"Jack, is there any news?" Grandma asked.

"Nothing worthwhile, ma." He, too, disappeared into the bedroom for the evening.

Moments later an ungainly figure in brown habit plodded into the doorway. Slowly the veiled gaze roved around the room and settled on Bandit. "You're not supposed to have him in here," said a voice from the white, flaccid face framed in iron curls.

Roman and Michael looked at each other and back to the apparition.

"Sister Helen, is that you?" asked Grandma.

The figure drew back. "Miss Margaret?!"

"Yes, Helen, these are my grandsons and their dog."

"Oh... I see... well... I hope you're not staying long." She vanished.

Settling slowly from their confusion, the boys sat together some time longer until the bedroom door opened a crack and a cracked whispered summoned them to sleep. Grandma and Uncle Joe stayed without, unmoved.

It took Roman an hour to fall asleep. Several times he nearly drifted off, but again and again he realized sleep's nearness and, in the realization, roused himself. At last he dreamed, blindly at first, of a piercing pain in his left palm. Lifting it to his growing vision he saw among the familiar creases the dull brassy curve of a great fishhook; turning his hand over he saw the point and barb brightened with blood, and as he watched, the hook twitched. He then discerned the line, a fine golden braid so light and tense as to convey intact each impulse it received. He knew then that there was much more to the landscape but refused his eyes' desire to stray from the golden thread. Following it to its end, half-expecting to find there some mad fisherman, he was instead engulfed by a green eye, and in its surface his own sight expanded so that now he saw the sea, grey and wild, and Francis, whirling on the harsh crests, his right palm pierced as Roman's. Roman, immobile, looked down upon a seawall, also grey, its stairs immersed in the swollen sea that lashed his legs, aching as if from day-long exertion.

Through his stupefied impressions shot again, again, wonder that it was he and not Francis perched on the relative safety of the seawall. The pain broke through his wondering then, the pain in his palm and in his calves and in his right hand wound round and round with the line as he fought to bring his friend to shore. His brain moved about the scene, assessing each second's play and the disasters of an ill-timed tug. He felt, without knowing how, that the fault in Francis's predicament lay with him, and he knew, too, that however well he performed now the cold waves might yield his friend up dead.

Roman woke then and thought for a moment that he had gone blind, a sense in which he might have persisted were it not for its having come upon him once before in a secluded cabin in Mississippi. Waking up without the glow of streetlights against the blinds, unable to discern the faintest shape or shade, he had believed, unable to entertain any other possibilities, that sight had deserted him, believed it until, groping his way to the restroom and frantically flicking on the yellow light above the mirror, he had seen his own staring eyes. Soothed by memory and nonetheless still blind, he began to notice the hard hammering of rain on the roof and its amplification at the wild whips of wind that roused a creaking chorus from the pines' wet, scaly spines. The air, cooler, had stilled and grown stale in the room. Roman sensed that he was not alone in his wakefulness.

The bedroom door opened slowly, and a figure edged its way through the thin aperture.

"Jack, what's going on?" rose his mother's hoarse voice.

"Power's out."

"I knew this would happen!" Michael whispered with glee, reaching deftly for the pocket of his vest, hung on the headboard against the eventuality, and flicking on his smaller flashlight. Eight eyes tightened in the sudden glow. "Deal with it, Rome."

"Anything on the radio?" Roman asked, assuming his father had crept out to listen for news in his truck.

"We're in the worst of it now. They're saying the storm jogged right at the last minute, so hopefully we dodged a bullet. Everything's holding up so far."

His father's words moved silently about his mind as Roman tried to fall asleep again, stifled by the still air and unwillingly attuned to his mother's discomfort. Whenever in the following years Roman heard his father tell the story of those days, he heard those same terms: "jogged right," "dodged a bullet," terms which conveyed personhood on the city--huge, obdurate, cemented in its own syrup and still miraculously agile in the manner of the fool--as well as on the storm--murderous and nimble and deceptive. The storm performed the offices of its villainous apotheosis; it would be left to those who exalted it and suffered its brief deity to work a resurrection.

iii

Thus the impulse of our myth.

The day the levees broke was long and gray and cool and existed mostly on the long blue balconies of the hotel and in groups huddled around tiny television sets plugged into car adapters. It wasn't until the worst of the storm had passed that the worst of its work began, and it was on one of those small and static-shot screens that Roman watched as the yacht club, just across the harbor from the Point, burned. The sea had risen far above that land outside the levee and in the sheets of rain shimmering in the electrical flames it seemed to merge with the sky so that it was only the rising fire that gave gravity to the scene, the scene which for Roman symbolized the shattering of the gates. His uncle managed the club, and Roman had spent countless summer evenings in its long dining room above the sea; though it would be rebuilt he would never enter it again. He wondered as he watched the blaze about Calvin and whether he remained at the Point, sleeping undisturbed in the bed of his truck.

Three hours later the wall of the Seventeenth Street Canal had broken, and the Morans watched in astonishment as the waters flowed interminably into their streets. None of them wept at the time; Roman waited, amazed, for the tears that never came.

The days in the storm's wake seemed miraculously bright, and perhaps it was this luxuriance of late summer which cast the time so finely in Roman's mind. Perhaps, again, it was that here, for once, he had broken with, or rather been driven from, the rut rehearsed for him by generations. He experienced in those days an intensity of presence which of necessity brightens circumstance. Expectations for the future changed daily, and it was youth's prerogative not to lay what plans could be laid. Perhaps, having felt himself in cold, distant orbit at Ignatius, he found himself now invested with the full power of those rings whose authority he had felt at the announcement of the storm's approach: the ring of those affected by the storm; the narrower of those displaced; the narrower still of those who had lost everything not packed into two cars.

The situation of the hotel, too, ensured that Roman and Michael would not want entertainment in those days. They crafted fishing rods from bamboo canes and tackle forgotten in their father's truck and caught bluegill and bass in the creek and the golf course ponds. They played basketball and ran mile after mile on the treadmills in the fitness center. They spoke now and then with the other children, all exultant in a strange sense of mastery.

The timeless days were interminable, on the other hand, for Roman's mother. Her husband, after innumerable phone conferences on the themes of ATVs, chainsaws, and artillery, had left to seek out incommunicant family nearer New Orleans, and she was left to oversee the maintenance of the rest of the family. Power had not returned to the hotel, and after the storm's cool air had passed, the days had grown still, wet, and warm. Grandma asked forever, or Eloise at least thought she did, for ice, while Uncle Joe, attended by the border collie's piteous brown gaze, moaned on the balcony. Neither, to her half-ashamed comfort, would join her in the cool air of her car, where she spent long hours in conversation with her sisters and, it must be assumed, in hurried and rather desperate prayer.

Soon, though, Jack returned, dirty and tired but bearing reassuring news of his relations. Soon, too, it became clear that the hotel's power would not return at any near date. They left, then, somewhat regretfully in Roman's case, and drove to Lafayette, where they deposited Grandma and Uncle Joe with some rather distant and very confused cousins, and then to Dallas, where most of Eloise's family had gathered.

As out of the hot Texas night the Dallas skyline arose, at first a faint sphere slowly swelling to a world of metal and money flooding from flats of scrub oak and mesquite rooted in the ruins of Precambrian seas, Roman was struck by a skyscraper outlined in green lights. Gazing on it for some minutes, he took up again the copy of *The Temple of Gold* in his lap and read in the brightening film of light pressing upon his window. One of his teachers had assigned the book and though he need not have read it, it had drawn him on through the day by some alien power.

Soon the Morans vanished into the slow breath of the city's evening, and a pair of smiling, astonished, black-hatted valets took command of their overladen cars at the Fairmont's burnished brass doors. In view of their plight their room was assigned gratis, and the border collie had the pleasure of riding seventeen floors every six hours to urinate on a patch of grass across the street from the lobby. For Eloise it was somehow comforting simply to stand so high above any water; she spent hours of the following days staring into the benign and bustling air, her eye drawn again, again to the spire of the cathedral. There, too, she spent hours, drinking comfort from the cool, concordant symmetry of its vast nave, from its spare Aztecan opulence, and from the dappled plashing of its font.

They moved after a few days to a more modest hotel in a Dallas suburb, then to another, each shift entailing its endless drill of loading and unloading for fear that the little left should be stolen. Sweat came quickly, yet it seemed in that drier air to vanish almost as it appeared.

In the interludes they visited Eloise's family, a dozen or so of Roman's cousins and the attendant aunts, uncles, and grandmother, all lodged in the same North Dallas hotel. By day the children raced about the hotel hallways until, predictably chastised by proprietor or patron, they adjourned to a baseball field across the street. Once they ventured to the Galleria, where they slipped noisily about the ice rink's narrow pound. Each evening they swam in the courtyard as the adults lounged and gave Sicilian vent to their several musings.

It was good to swim, though Roman, glancing up from the pool at the walls of windows on all sides, wondered what eyes were upon them. And his sense of presence was borne out by the frequent cobalt stare of a man who had by some means attached himself to their party, a refugee who spent the evenings with the adults and seemed, if with some shade of unease, to mix comfortably with them. Roman could not hold his eye.

After a week of this, whether from some sudden wish for solitude or sickness with the dust and heat and the blue stare or simply from a dislocated recklessness, they had driven to Georgia to hike and fish at a resort they'd visited once with

Francis's family. The air was cooler, and in the mornings a faint mist flamed above the lake. Going down to the dock one evening they met the proprietor, a man near sixty, very round about the middle, with lank grey hair limping from beneath his cap and thick glasses that blurred and magnified his eyes.

While Jack inquired after a rental for the following morning, the boys climbed a stone bridge stretching over the boathouse canal to a small island, its gravel paths banked in hibiscus, azalea, and rose. Studying the water from the arch, they discerned the dim shapes of massive bluegills finning in slow rounds. The man, in turn, made his inquiries, and learning of their loss, turned a disconsolate gaze on the boys. His jaw had gone slack with tragedy's impress, and his limp jowls trembled. The blurred eyes blurred further.

He offered to take the family to dinner, to let his wife cook for them that night, desperate to do something for their suffering. Jack, moved, nonetheless refused, whether from a reluctance to be bound or a proud reticence he himself could not have said. Not to be vanquished the man finally demanded they accept a free rental the next morning as well as some of his own rods and reels. He asked, finally, what they wanted to catch, and when they said mainly bluegill concluded, "Yep, y'all are just like me. Just like me."

In the morning, however, they found the little booth, its dim yellow bulb harsh against the argent twilight, possessed not by their misericordial acquaintance but rather by a younger man who knew nothing of the last evening's arrangement. Caught between sympathy and self, he shuffled papers about the desk, smiling and apologizing until Jack said not to worry about it, that they would simply pay.

They had nosed out of the boathouse into the thin mist and had just begun to cast to the banks of the little floral island when shouts rose up after them. Turning they watched with no little amusement as the man from the previous evening, a dozen rods in hand, trundled down the steps to the boathouse.

With a curt curse en passant for his young colleague, he suddenly appeared at the round head of the island, forcing apologies between wheezes. He seemed, whether by communication or intuition, to have grasped the situation and cast imprecations repeatedly over his shoulder. The Morans should have struggled not to disembark with laughter had the man's manner been less abject. As it was, they assured him over the course of some minutes that they bore no one ill will in the matter; graciously they accepted the loan of three rods. Finally, after repeating that they were just like him, he turned, muttering and slowly shaking his head, back toward the mainland, and the Morans motored to quieter waters. The fishing was fine, yet even as Roman brought the largest bluegill of his life over the gunwale he felt himself gripped by a new melancholy at the thought of the boatman's sympathy.

On the following day they returned to Dallas, and the question of schooling, one Roman and Michael had studiously avoided, arose and obstinately floated. No authority could say when the boys' schools, both yet flooded, would open again. It was decided, then, that Eloise would teach Michael in their hotel room and that Roman would attend the Jesuit school in Dallas, a svelte edifice much more modern than the one in New Orleans, clean and arrayed in exemplary works of contemporary sculpture and painting, all abstract. Just as their registration was completed, Fr. Muller announced the establishment of a sort of Ignatius Prep colony on the campus of its Houston counterpart. Once more they moved.

It was during the drive South, in the middle of a hot, cloudless September day, that Roman heard at last from Francis. There were many long days in the car that month, Roman in the Suburban with his mother, Michael in the truck with his father. Sitting in the back row of the SUV through frequent hours of silence, Roman regularly permitted his thoughts to wander into unwonted regions of license which, together with the rhythmic movements of the highway and his hands, set into motion his body's swelling plants and factories. They marked one of the few smudges of unease on the events of the month, these periods of sharp self-arousal halted by the desperate strain of deep reservations tapering off over long and uncomfortable hours. It was thus with a begrudging gratitude turning to relief that he heard the phone ring.

His mother, glancing at her phone, answered volubly, "Hey Clara!"

Francis's mother, then. As he awaited the phone's certain conveyance a curious unease came over Roman. He attributed it to a long-standing privacy in his friendships, though he sensed some other, more novel cause beside; when at length the phone was extended toward him he reached for it, stretching across the middle seat, with some measure of reluctance.

"Hello?"

"Hey, bud!"

"Hey, how's it going?"

"It's alright. You?"

"Pretty good."

"Where are y'all?"

"Somewhere between Dallas and Houston. So did y'all evacuate?"

"Yeah, right at the last minute we went to that old lake house. Took eight hours to get there."

"Geez. Was that far enough away?"

"Not really. A pine tree fell on the porch."

"Man. What are you doing for school?"

"East Feliciana High." (He had assumed a twang).

"*Public* school?"

"Ohhh, very public." His voice trailed off at the end as though displaced by some telling memory. "Yeah, it's pretty different. Like the other night we went to get pizza and a bunch of kids from school were there, and one of them was wearing a shirt that just said 'Viagra,' so he walked to our table and said, 'Hey Frank, like my shirt?' and walked away. My mom lost it."

Roman laughed, somewhat nervously, and looked askance at his mother in the mirror, her eyes inscrutable behind sunglasses. Francis had in recent years faded in her estimation. She, for one, would not have lost it at such dysfunction. Of course she shouldn't have been able to hear, yet her ears were at times supernaturally sharp, as once when in the dead of night she'd woken up at the sound of a cockroach scuttling across the carpet in her closet.

Francis, perhaps from an accurate interpretation of his friend's pause, continued, "What about you?"

"Well, looks like I'm gonna go to the Jesuit school in Houston. Any idea when y'all'll be back in New Orleans."

"I don't know. Not for a while still. My dad's not sure we will go back."

"Why?"

"I don't know, they just think it's a big risk."

Again Roman paused.

"Hey, my mom needs the phone back. Glad you're safe."

"Me too."

Two hours later the Morans checked into a hotel in Houston, and the now familiar drill began again of hauling clothes, the dog, the twenty years of photo albums up from the parking lot. This done, they variously rested, read, and watched the news, still roiling with flood footage. As they strained for a glimpse of their house, Jack's phone rang. He answered, said yes he could talk, and after a minute went out into the hall, deflecting the dog's curiosity by a deft foot to the nose.

Presently he returned and asked immediately if they were hungry. Eagerly the boys arose. Eloise looked intently at him, and he as intently avoided her eye. As they set off through the sprawling and shadeless streets the nerves twitched at her tongue. It was then about noon.

She was surprised to find that Roman's eyes and ears kept pace with hers. A car seemed angling toward them from the next lane; just as her lips parted, she heard Roman say, "Dad, watch out!" Michael, gazing on the urban vastness, popped his tongue again, again against his bottom teeth. Roman supplied the necessary "Michael!" Her anxiety, denied any outlet, swelled, and she began to press her feet alternately against the floor of the car. Jack's silence hardened, and she glanced tensely toward him every several seconds.

After some minutes of wandering through the scene of endless similitude, they came upon a sort of deli, which stood out in virtue of a shade of originality. Jack pulled into the lot, took two bills from his wallet, and handed them to Roman. "Y'all go get us something."

"What do you..." Michael began, but Roman, sensing strife, said sharply, "Michael, come on. We'll figure it out."

Entering the cool, sunlit restaurant, Roman lingered some paces from the counter, studying the menu with uncommon diligence. Michael, having taken in its contents at a glance, turned an increasingly confused eye toward him.

The cashier, having stepped expectantly to the counter, now said, "Just holler when y'all're ready."

Roman, meeting her eye for a moment, responded, feeling rather stupid, "Ok, yeah, we're from out of town."

Half afraid, he glanced through the double pane of storefront and windshield. His stomach tightened as he saw his father crying, not violently but with a depth of dejection plain even twice removed. Never before had he witnessed his father's tears, though it was said that he wept at the miscarriage of his first child. And there came to him the harrowing thought, even as he stepped toward the counter, that the maw of miscarriage might gape yet far beyond the womb, that it lay far or near in the grave's broken teeth through the sweat and shrieking of the rolling world.

Addressing the cashier, he began at last to order, haltingly and with myriad questions. Michael, oblivious, gaped and then began to laugh at this sudden fit of idiocy. Finally, the cashier having unraveled his convolutions and turned away, lightly shaking her head, Roman whirled on his giggling brother, seized his shoulder and squeezing it hissed, "Would you shut up! Do you have any idea what's going on?"

Michael, hurt as swiftly as amused, shook free and cast down his brimming gaze. Immediately, though with slight annoyance, Roman felt the blood in his ears. Stepping closer to Michael he said, more softly, embarrassed by intimacy, "I'm sorry, buddy. I just think something's wrong with mom and dad, so that's why I wanted to take our time."

Together they glanced outside again and saw their parents' faces both inclined, their mother's hand on their father's shoulder. They seemed to speak in soft dejection.

Soon the smirking cashier handed Roman a large white paper bag, and the two boys stepped out into the humid light. Their parents glanced up, calm again, though the traces of their father's tears did not escape even Michael's notice. The quiet car filled quickly with the scents of fresh bread, butter, cheese, and meat; hunger swelled in the silence.

"Rome, you got any change for me?"

"Oh yeah," Roman reached into his pocket, withdrew two crumpled ones and scattered coins and handed them forward.

"Two dollars?"

"Well, I got eight sandwiches."

"What for?" his father asked, but all of them had begun to laugh.

"We're not gonna make it on one sandwich."

"Ok, fats."

"Don't say that," Eloise broke in, sharp but smiling.

They continued in this manner through the evening. Ponderous questions mingled with their lighter thoughts, yet they'd reached a point in the day when nothing more practical might be done.

All the same, when the night had deepened and the rest of his family slept peacefully, Roman lay awake on the green, uncomfortable couch in the sitting room of their suite. Before him yawned evidently endless possibility, tired of the nervous joy of life derailed.

iv

It was not alone that he lived in crisis. The third morning after the storm saw Stephen LaCour paddling a well-worn canoe of bright wood through the courtyard of Ignatius Prep. It was quiet, save for the distant throb of helicopters, and the air remained unseasonably cool in the storm's wake. The brown water had yet to exalt its stench. On a whim he passed through the upper branches of an oak tree, disturbing a red-eared slider, which vanished almost without a ripple beneath the still turbid water. Turning again to business, Stephen directed his craft down the length of the school building and, finding just enough water beneath him to clear the courtyard gate, passed on into the glare of Palmyra Street.

Feast them upon the wideness of the sea.

On his left as he turned northward lay a shining expanse of still water beneath which drowned the green school field. Here at its edge he felt faint currents gently pressing at the hull of his canoe and at the blade of the smooth wooden paddle. To his right passed the pageantry of mid-city upper story windows, glazed in pastels various as taste. He considered the shrimp plants in the gardens below him, imagining their pink blossoms flicking free and joining the life of their crustacean genus. Then from the subaqueous flickering he rose in thought to the astral flame beyond the mantling sky and to whatever souls might wander there, whether in their own measures of distress or some unfallen ease.

Presently he turned up St. Patrick toward Canal and, reaching a three-story aquamarine house, pulled up to its second-floor balcony, grasped its rail and in a fluid motion boarded his home. He tied off the canoe to the railing, dug a key from the dirt at the roots of a potted pepper plant, and let himself in.

He knew, assuming no looters had come, precisely where the things he wished would lie: on the top shelf of the mahogany case, just between Blake and Keats, the old volume of Hopkins, highest relic of his Duke days; on the broad desk of unvarnished oak, beside his neatly stacked stationery, the fountain pen, his father's, in continual use since the latter's passage; a bit of concrete hidden at the back of the desk drawer.

This last piece, a fragment of the Coliseum collected in a vagrant summer some decades before, accompanied him in all journeys. It served as memento of his martyrdom. He had been on the verge of marrying when a fundamental melancholy warned him of something amiss. So he had made his excuses and left. For a time he'd poked about Ireland, mostly in the neighborhood of Cork. Then to Oxford, where he'd clung to the Isis and the punting company of its swans and an inebriate band of undergraduates. Then Bruges, Paris, Provence, Valencia for a moment and on to Morocco, where in Casablanca he'd encountered an old acquaintance and so come to Rome. The acquaintance, as it developed, was an oaf;

he supplied the perfect proof of his oafishness on a visit to the Coliseum. After loitering about the grim, vine-grown arcades they had both grown bored, and as they peered about into gloomy galleries for some secret scene of violence or lust they came to a bright and quiet corner. Seeing a fist-sized chunk of concrete loose the acquaintance had seized it and cracked it free. That day the two parted ways, but Stephen, having seen a bit of the stone rattle to the pavement near the Forum, had not scrupled to take it.

With a last unsentimental glance about the room he stepped back out along the balcony and into his bark, glad again of his solitude. Paddling back to the brown building he cast discrete eyes into each quiet corner. With Fr. Muller and the three other Jesuits who, too, had ridden out the storm in their studious fastness, he had taken pains to ensure that no one desperate would learn of their presence in the water's midst. All lights had been extinguished after dark. Those who had stepped out onto the roof, edging around the rain-cool pool to survey the scene below, had done so in the night and with the utmost stealth.

Reaching the school's balcony again, Stephen tied off his canoe and joined the Jesuits within. Later that hour a large skiff, piloted by an Ignatius graduate of the '98 class, motored up to the second floor. The motley procession boarded and their captain, careful in spite of the obvious not to throw a wake upon the homes he passed, idled down Canal Street to an I-10 overpass, drawing as near the on-ramp as he could. Then Stephen and his company of black robes stepped off into the warm, knee-deep water. The two oldest had done no such thing in decades, and Stephen, glancing expectantly toward them, found them indeed smiling to themselves, their progress up the ramp slowed more by pleasure than age. Soon they joined the babbling masses in the shade of the interstate. The zealous ministered to the zealous; the quiet retired to an empty place; Stephen gossiped with a neighbor. Toward afternoon a bus arrived, gathered its capacity, and began its slow, simmering progress to Houston.

Stephen spent some few nights in a Jesuit house there, yet as the basic incommensurability of the single and the celibate life must assert itself sooner or later, he moved to a nearby hotel where, as it developed, two of his colleagues had likewise taken refuge. By day they explored the city's cultural offerings (with much attendant scoffing and discourse on the advance of barbarism); by night they appropriated the hotel bar's liberal resources, and here they scoffed not. Thus passed the week before responsibility returned to its post.

v

On the following Sunday, the second since the storm, Fr. Muller was one of the first people in Houston completely and purposefully awake. He made it a point always to rise before the Sun, and circumstance had further curtailed his sleep. By 4:04 he had showered and shaved. He had awoken with a sense for the day's homily and its skeleton lay assembled in his mind when by 4:10 he had completed the Office of Readings. He spent the next two hours drafting notes to faculty, families, contractors, Jesuits, friends, benefactors, alumni--in short, anyone connected with Ignatius Prep. He had been its president for nearly two decades now, an extraordinarily long tenure, and he was the only person not happy he had held the post for so long.

Initial estimates of damage to Ignatius ran upwards of five million dollars. Against a frantic storm of dissent he had decided, nonetheless, to retain all faculty at full salary, and he had arranged for about forty of them to join him in Houston, along with some three hundred displaced students. They would meet between 3:30 and nine, Sunday to Thursday, with as normal a classroom life as could be managed, beginning that afternoon with Mass.

The processional hymn began at 2:30. The homily began at 2:37 and ended at 2:40 and ran as follows:

"In Vergil's *Aeneid*, when relating the fall of Troy, Aeneas offers a remark well known to our Latin IV students. He says, 'Forsan et haec olim meminisse iuvabit. Perhaps some day it will be pleasing to remember even these things.' His is a sentiment we might each bear in mind today and through the days until we return to normal, though of course the events of these days will forever shape our new conception of what is normal.

"I've spoken regularly over the past years of two temptations we fall into too easily: self-pity and self-deception. The intersection of the two is deadly.

"Now more than ever we are tempted to pity ourselves, to take stock of our suffering and decide that we've had enough for a lifetime, to weigh God and find him wanting. Such a decision, of course, is merely a kind of self-deception, an attempt to arrogate to ourselves the power which belongs only to God. It's what the Israelites did immediately after God brought them safely out of Egypt, claiming they'd had it better with their flesh pots and onions.

"God has a plan for all of us. It's very hard to believe that the events of the past two weeks could be a part of that plan, but if we truly believe that God is good and loving, then we must believe that God is master of history, even if his mastery transcends our logical comprehension. We see only a small part of the spectrum of light. It may be that our minds comprehend only a small part of the spectrum of being.

"Let us pray today that God will give us the faith and hope to trust in his will and the charity to help others to trust as well."

vi

Father Muller's homily, appreciated by most for its brevity and by some for its content, had not been universally attended. A boy older than his stature suggested, darkly complected with a disarming shrewdness of glance, had slipped stealthily into a restroom just as that homily began. It was finely situated, this bathroom; he had selected it on a sort of scouting mission earlier that day. The storm had halted his career and probably effaced four years' delicate work, but he, Spencer Zazulak, remained undaunted. He opened the door of a clean corner stall, gingerly closed the lid of the toilet, took his seat, and went to work. Twenty minutes later he flushed, having carved into the wall something which had never before existed:

The Odyssey of the Craphouse Poet

Hurricanes killed me
and Houston billed me.
Still I'm still me.
My rhymes be ill, see?

For three weeks circumstance had denied Spencer's artistic daimon its usual mode of expression; sated for the moment, he walked into the hallway just as it filled with students fresh from their less singular communion.

vii

LaCour scanned each face filing past the unfamiliar desk into the broad room brightened by unhampered Houston sun. A jejeune air, perceptible perhaps to him alone, had stifled his typically lively sensibility throughout the afternoon, and he wondered as he watched the freckled capped or clear but always somehow smooth skin if in the great abnegation of the ties typical of his age he had become some watcher, node in the alluvial reticulum of the River, if somehow his malleable vivens had come at the cost of an eternal enframing.

The cure dispensed itself to him at its own discretion in the faces. Most of the class had entered by now, and a touch of his care lifted as those known to each other yipped and prodded while the new boys nosed gently into safe spaces. Here one, obviously Sicilian, eyed him in eager unease, a round white smile shining from the almond skin. Behind there came one tall for his age, swaying foot to foot, his eyes cast down as if in melancholic musing. In the early part of his career LaCour had read offense in such eyes. It had needed the better part of thirty years for him to learn the two truths he now repeated to himself as if in incantation, that hardly any boy he met truly hated anything, and second this despite the fact that many of them faced daily brokenness he could hardly conceive. Pondering the mills of his sin he said, "How we doing today, Sayre?"

The swaying boy looked up, startled.

"Pretty good, I guess," he said in a deep, perhaps self-conscious, voice.

"Alright, glad to have you." Sayre sat down, a dim red tinge in his clear pale cheeks, welcomed in his singling.

Some teachers would begin the day with speeches. Partly from his own acedic sense and a vague habit of spite but mainly from a desire simply for words LaCour passed over any such preamble and after a prefatory "Hail Mary" said in his empowered public tone, "Good afternoon, men! Today we're doing something you might not be used to. I've seen some of you laughing already at the sheet of paper on your desks. If you haven't already done so, or if you have, please read the poem there now."

Roman, seated halfway down the second row from the door, turned for the second time to "The Emperor of Ice Cream." In a new silence a tittering sussurus arose, scattered snickerings and suppressed breaths of sarcastic inquisition. Astonished eyes rose to LaCour's slow-revolving gaze, now impassive, now haughty, now amused. Just before the boys' confusion dispersed itself in uproar, LaCour, raising his voice again, asked, "Who can tell me what this poem means?"

In the renewed silence all hands were still. On several studious faces appeared the strain of need for an answer.

After some eight tense seconds LaCour said, "I'm so glad none of you said anything. I was getting ready to kill somebody. Let's try this instead: who can tell me something about ice cream?"

A dozen hands jumped.

"Bacques, whatcha got?"

"It's delicious."

"Absolutely, what else?"

"There are lots of flavors," offered another boy.

"Sure, sure, what are y'all's favorites?"

A chorus of contention swirled.

"Alright, alright," LaCour at last shouted, "we all know vanilla's the best."

"Nooooo! Booo! Come on!"

"Easy, men, easy! Now who can tell me something else about ice cream?"

"It melts," said Sayre.

"Very good. So here we've got ice cream, which is so sweet and so cold and comes in so many flavors, but it still melts. But what else is this poem talking about?"

Silence again, with now and then the rasp of skin along paper.

"Is someone dead?"

"Yes! Someone is dead. How'd you get that, Paquette?"

"Well, there's something about a sheet over someone and the horny [snickers] feet coming out. Is that like some kind of old person?"

"It is like some kind of old person, sure. So what's going on here? What's Stevens doing for us? There's some sort of fundamental comparison being drawn here. Anybody tell me what that is?"

"Is it pretty much ice cream and death?"

"Yes, or maybe ice cream and people, right? Because that's the thing about death, is that it doesn't melt, huh?"

A ghastly pageant had dimly shaped itself now in the more attentive minds about the room, memories of daily drives past graveyards where surely ran a constant sarcophagal melting, a cold and uncomposed dismantling and congealing.

"So let's get a little closer in now, and I wanna start with one line of the poem, 'Let be be finale of seem.' Everybody see that? 'Let be be finale of seem.' That line is the whole reason I gave you this poem today. I read it when I was just a little older than y'all and said 'what the hell is this guy talking about?' But sure enough it stuck in my head somewhere and then years later something would happen and all the sudden I'd think 'that's it!' But I've never gotten to the end of it. There's always something more, something that makes you wake up in the middle of the night thinking that's it, too. Hopefully at least one of you'll know what I mean someday."

For the rest of the period the class, enthralled as well by some sense of novel largesse as by LaCour's captivation, pored in pairs over the text, offering commentary over a broad spectrum of incision. LaCour dismissed nothing entire and wove from their observations as compelling a gloss on the poem as might be had in a room of boys of fourteen.

Roman's quiet insights, as for instance about the nature of empire or the poem's slippery metric, bore a pedestrian and analytic character. It was in the realms of biology and mathematics that he had always felt most at home and in which he had professed his future. Now, though, he felt the first fine stirring of a love different though perhaps at root indistinct, as if he had reached beneath a sheet, lightly fluttering, and felt the touch of something infinitely powerful which yet vanished at his grasp.

viii

Thus began one of the most unusual parts of Roman's life, a transmutation of all that was normal effected by a slight shift in place and time. For of course the teachers, students, and courses were the same, but instead of lunch the boys ate dinner, and instead of walking out of the building into the amber afternoons of late September, they walked out into the Houston night, heavy with the thunder of highways and the hum of expanding life.

Roman remained a part of that loose crowd in Houston for just three weeks, at which time Fr. Muller announced his establishment of a second satellite location at a Methodist high school just outside of New Orleans, and as Roman's father was anxious to return to the city, it was decided that he would start the school year once more there. These three weeks would therefore have passed largely without consequence if not for his meeting Molly the day before he departed.

A girls' high school stood next door to Houston's Berchmanns Prep, and the girls, in something of the fashion of the USO, came occasionally to socialize with the refugees. One evening Roman sat on the edge of a group of boys with whom he'd become slightly acquainted, eating quietly as they discussed movies.

"Look, all I'm saying is that *Dirty Harry* is definitely better than *Pale Rider*."

"And all I'm saying is that to compare two movies in different genres is to commit a foul of the most asinine character."

"Alright, Taylor, you wanna talk asinine—how about claiming that Clint Eastwood is anything other than a genre in himself? How's that for asinine?"

Such contention had come to define for Roman the character of his classmates' conversation. Again and again arguments intensified as the slightest of issues took on apparently infinite importance by reference to opinion and personality.

As the battle raged, a girl about his age entered the cafeteria. Her dark hair curled in wild array above her pearlescent oval face. Black eyebrows streaked her high forehead, and her large, dark eyes seemed on the verge of laughter. She disappeared before his observations could go further, and then, suddenly and inexplicably, she was seated across the table from him. They had never met, he was not at that time handsome, his morose air not what he should have thought welcoming.

"Mind if I sit here?"

"Not at all."

"Great. I'm Molly."

"Roman."

"What else?"

"What else what?"

"What's the rest of your name?"

"Moran."

"Middle?"

"Schiro."

"Ah, so some sort of Pythagorean anagram then, huh? You really shouldn't be eating those," she added, gesturing to his plate. It was Monday, and in honor of its new inmates the cafeteria had prepared red beans.

He stared at her, and she continued, "You know, Greek by Sicily and so on."

"Well, I don't really know about that. I just know it was my great-grandfather's name. Don't know why I got it. They say he was a real jerk."

"Maybe you're the redeemer. And anyway it's such a lovely name."

"Well, thanks." From the corner of his eye he felt his classmates' attention. Intent on holding his advantage he cast about for topics. "I like your earrings." He had noticed a pair of rich blue pendants in perfect counterpoint to her black hair and her brilliant teeth, which were somehow attractively large. He hadn't thought; presently he blushed.

"Oh, thanks! They're lapis lazuli, like Yeats. 'Heaven blazing into the head' you know."

His face made it plain he did not know, and so she continued, "Well, you of all people at least ought to know about 'Tragedy wrought to its uttermost.' Did your family lose much?"

"Almost everything." He briefly but thoroughly related the events of the preceding weeks to her. She listened attentively, her eyes slightly darkened. He spoke with an unreserve which amazed him when that evening he again and again revisited their conversation. Whether because he assumed he would never again speak to her or because of some heightened receptivity she conveyed, she was the first person his age with whom he'd spoken freely in a month.

"Have you found it good to suffer?" she asked when he concluded.

"Why would I?"

"Oh, I don't know. But it's supposed to be better at least than making people suffer."

"Mm. Honestly I haven't thought about it too much, but I guess I've been happier lately than it seems like I should be. Does that make sense?"

"You're a regular Socrates."

"How do you know all this?" He should normally have burned with jealousy, but her manner precluded such a response and roused instead a happy curiosity.

"There's one elective class, but I've mostly learned about it from my dad. He's a professor. He teaches in Rome right now, so I don't see him very often, but we write letters. Here."

She pulled a creased envelope from her small blue purse, withdrew from it a sheet the shade of yellowed marble, and handed it across the table to him. He eyed it doubtfully, but she urged him to read.

"Nothing good really needs to be private. Go on."

Still hesitant, Roman unfolded the missive and read its contents, written in a clean and flourishing script:

Dearest Molly:

No doubt there would be little advantage to the soul *sub specie aeternitatis* if we stopped at a merely Aristotelian understanding, if, that is, pure thought alone survived death. In a fulfilled Peripateticism, though, we understand God not as simple self-reflection but as self-reflection revealed in Trinity, Creation, and Incarnation, the character of divinity being to go where God is not (you understand I write somewhat equivocally here).

Now, if God is love and if the soul is meant for God, then it follows that marriage, as image of Trinitarian love, is the finest (and so necessarily the hardest) preparation for heavenly contemplation. This assumes, of course, a sacramental understanding of marriage and an understanding of all human loves as subordinate to divine Love.

The Resurrection, of course, if not simply the Incarnation, gives the lie to Aristotle's dismissal of all but active intellect, and this resolves the fear that any human relationship would be irrevocably forfeit in death. To be sure, though, the marriage bond would be subsumed into the deeper bond of the heavenly marriage.

I'm curious to hear your take on this—if any objections might remain. The important thing is to find a spouse who reflects the Father to you. But for most of us that spousal love begins in our friends. Think of the way you and Anna have grown up together, the other always there, always the best friend and understood to be no matter what.

I miss you and mother dearly. Autumn is fast approaching here, and I wish you both could stomp the grapes with me. The students are in fine form; they seem a sharper bunch than the typical Fall crowd. I hope you'll spend a semester here soon.

Love always,

Daddy

Roman had rarely before encountered anyone who knew very clearly what or why to believe. Here he briefly glimpsed a breadth and surety of understanding which disclosed the corner of a deep desire within himself to believe and know.

Molly looked at him expectantly, plainly amused at the confusion evident on his face.

"Any questions?"

"I wouldn't know where to start."

"Well, then, we'll have plenty to talk about."

"I wish we could, but I'm actually going back to New Orleans tomorrow."

"Oh. Well, why don't you keep the letter and the envelope and write me?"

He looked at her for a moment, sensing despite her evidently genuine cheer an uncertain sadness. "Can't I just call you?"

"Nope. You have to write me if you want to stay in touch." And Roman was astonished to find suddenly that she was gone, leaving behind the shadow of a scent he would come to know years later as verbena.

ix

His dinner conversation had left Roman with a slightly altered estimation of himself, though shifts of that type occur with startling rapidity at such an age. Later in the evening, as he crossed the green darkness of the campus, warm with the walks' slow cooling and his own reflection, he came upon a group of older students. As he drew nearer, he saw how large they were. One especially stood out, a mountainous presence on the borderland of his roving riot of companions. He seemed the subject of their raucous conversation, and as they came level with Roman one of them said, "Yeah, Cameron eats eighth graders."

Here Cameron's slow gaze turned to encompass Roman. From the depths of his almost motionless mouth came the just articulated grunt, "You mean like that guy?" And with that he threw his left hand against Roman's shoulder, knocking him nearly from his feet as he stumbled into the grass along the breezeway.

Glancing around as he hurried on, he trembled with a sudden sense of shame, as though his soul had slipped out, caroused unseen amid the older boys' mirth, and taken pitiful stock of his body. Arriving in his Latin classroom he was met with general uproar, a mix of natural delight in the day's end and of the anticipated return to New Orleans and of a boyish pleasure in the company of LaCour, who'd been assigned the class by one of the strange permutations of the time acting on his own high school experience. Some part of him whispered to Roman, though he knew the causes of his classmates' laughter, that they were watching him, that word of his disgrace had spread across campus. At last, though, class began, and turning his attention to the second declension he felt once more at ease.

As LaCour saw it, ease had crossed its bounds that evening. He was one of three faculty going home the following morning, and whether from a redoubled sense of entrenchment or anxiety at an uncreated world he had felt an unwonted petulance prizing open his mind as the day had passed. Each dawdling gaze and unlooked-for word called a sharp reproof from his tongue. Finally, on a swell of chatter from behind his declining back, he ceded the position, and whirling about with chalk and Wheelock in hand and reddened eyes wide shouted, "JUST SHUT UP! OK? JUST SHUT! UP!" His voice tore over the final two words as he cracked Wheelock's spine over the edge of the podium.

A silence of fear, slight though genuine. The sense of embarrassment, slightly sickened, stole over Roman once again and stayed through the last quiet minutes of class.

When the bell chimed the boys filed out in sullen order, and LaCour followed, as chastened as they. Roman's parents awaited him at the edge of the block of classrooms, and LaCour, seeing them, approached. "These ya parents, Roman?"

"Yessir," and turning toward his parents, "This is Mr. LaCour."

"Stephen LaCour," he said, shaking their hands in turn.

"Ohhh, Roman talks about you all the time!" said his mother, ever eager before authority. "That's amazing that you can teach English and Latin!"

"Well, it's mostly the boys doing the work. You've got a great kid, by the way, absolute pleasure to teach." He turned a warm eye to Roman, who smiled, mostly mollified. "So I guess I'll see y'all at St. Paul's, then."

"Oh, are you going back?"

"Yep, one of the fortunate few."

"Well, good, see you there then."

And they separated, leaving the mesquite beneath which they'd stood to continue its curling in silence.

X

Having taken his last hotel shower for some months, Roman stood in a towel before the sink, examining his image through the warm mist. Again, he was without himself, and a distant wonder and disgust mingled at the fresh sight of unbidden change. In the translucent light of the shower he had noticed the new pallor of his skin, so lately dark with days of angling. He now studied for the first time a proliferation of hair, transfixed in particular by a wiry strand curling like a black question mark from a freckle on his left shoulder. In the mirror's hard glance its hooked end whitened, and in the face of this refinement its total coarseness intensified. At a sudden impulse he razed it, relieved the blade found in it no distinction. He turned then to the soft brown hairs around his nipples and there, gently, pressing taut the skin with his left hand, brought the razor to bear again, the skin puckering slightly at the blade's rough grip. Though the door was locked he had feared he might be found at this strange shearing, and he relaxed somewhat when it was finished.

Odd though the body might be, he found as he raised his eyes to themselves that the face had in some ways improved. Its rondure had taken shape in the summer heat, and the strong lines and curves of cheek and jaw made themselves known. Against them, too, the nose, which in its aquilinity yet gave its interlocutors a too strong sense of the future, took on at last a kind of congruity. The eyes, he had rejoiced to find earlier in the year, were not in fact brown as he had so long thought but rather a shade of hazel fraught with discs of gold. For a moment he studied them and then, peering briefly on the image entire in his pupils, turned away and dressed and slept.

III.

WITH THE WATER AS A WALL

Then eight, both, in the grey month to the manger, returning with gifts to the back yard to play, play as well as two could alone; and when they neared in the cold gray air, pursuant and pursued, came the scent of the house and the stale top bunk and the pale peculiar odor of himself.

And then the other kicked his quick vengeance and he seized as slowly, inexorably, it soared above the fence. Then they thawed and followed through the neighbor's triplet fencing, cobblestoned and choked by vines stilled a winter's minute in their killing. And the tool shed stood in its disuse a foot above the concrete slab and there on a cat's carcass of two weeks, first as if sleeping and then sickening as the orange and white striped coat blackened with buzzing punctuations, lay the new ball.

And then he nearly raged and would have had it been warmer but already it was gone despite this, this impossible except by some colossal mischance or maleficence. And he thought as they slumped along the gravel, stripping coats against the sudden sweat that this, the unconceived cradling in the dead cat's pelvis, should serve somehow as emblem.

i

For two weeks the flood waters remained, cupped by levees and the city's imperceptible declivities, stewing in summer's late long days. At last the overrun pumps ground awake and for three days vomited into the sea. Then, like demons into a swept house, flooded frenzied patrols of police and firemen, the National Guard and Red Cross: shifting fallen trees, guarding against thieves, above all sifting the swollen homes for the stranded and marking the doors of the dead. Two weeks into the harrowing, select school officials, among other authorities, were granted brief admittance to the city. First in the long queue at City Park Avenue was Fr. Muller. The policeman at the checkpoint had been one of his Greek pupils (and there he had distinguished himself by his sole and candid ignorance of Oedipus' fate) and had waved him on with only a smile. Along with a contractor he examined the wreckage, and by noon of that day he had arranged to have the first floor gutted and a new heating and cooling system installed. The work would not be completed until Thanksgiving at the earliest.

Not a man of sentiment, he was nonetheless moved at the sight of his soiled, stinking mother; before his mind's eye rode the Babylonian whore. And the rites of purification fell squarely to him. However, he had done all one could, so he drove immediately back to Houston. By the time he reached his hotel, he had mentally composed his sermons for the following week.

ii

Evidently ill-content with its prior efforts, the still unsettled Gulf lashed itself again in the torment of storm which, choosing its pilgrim path with sequel leisure, set a course for Galveston, so that now, curiously, even as Fr. Muller returned to his megalopolitan redoubt, the Morans were driven back to New Orleans. As they passed for the last time in many years through Houston's glutted, rushing heart, almost desert but for the bald punctuations of buildings like skeletal fingers forced from the earth, Roman struggled to conceive the scene in flood. Yet it had a month earlier required equal contortions to envision the ruin of his own city, and he ceded the imagination its swift, impoverished syllogism.

Roman's father had returned to New Orleans a day earlier. His brother managed a prominent shipping interest and, free himself to access the city, had agreed to bring Jack into the disaster area to assess the damage to his house. Eloise, left to see the children and the dog safely home, presently found herself locked into a car's length of Houston highway by the mad calculus of commute and evacuation.

After a moment the stillness and the sense of heat settled into her mind, which moved unhesitatingly into its most sinister region, the half-memory of seizure in the CT scanner, the dulled beat of blood to her brain and the incorrigible violence of the limbs. Her breath quickened and sweat expanded in the inscrutable hairs along her lip. By some secret store of strength, perhaps beyond her own, she refrained from shrieking, leaping from her seat, and careering down the endless ranks of burning cars. Yet the heat led to gentler thoughts, the girlhood memory of cracking eggs on the sidewalk with her sisters and of the mutual delight in shared scolding for the consequent lost cake. The blood smoothed her face once more, pressed the skin softly from her skull, and a quiet stream of tears relieved some portion of her burden of nerves. The boys dozed.

At last they began to move, first in short and slowly lengthening rolls and then in scurrying bursts until incredibly they roared on alone. Their journey assumed an almost clandestine character, the timbre of the secret orders into taken territory, when at the state line a sign had flashed its orange notice: NO VACANCIES STATE OF LOUISIANA. The news took on a dire significance in Eloise's mind. She would in later years frequently produce this detail to underline the terror of the time. Never mind that a house, on lend from one of Jack's friends, awaited them. Never mind that she never need go into the flood zone. Never mind the dead. The state had reached capacity, and she drove for the heart of it, where power still was unrestored and the night sky burned black and empty; the heart where, the rumors said, looters, ravenous dogs, and even wild boars, flushed from the surrounding swamps, pillaged at will; where one might well find corpses in the attic, baking.

She drove on toward this dark mass, increasingly peopled by the hoards in her imagination, and wept. The boys gazed out across the swamp, wondering what beasts bristled in its teeming waste.

After ten hours they arrived at their temporary home, a comfortable two-story in West Metairie. The boys knew the house well, for its owner, Simon Tan, had been a prominent benefactor in their young careers as outdoorsmen. Frequently the Morans had met Simon on the curb before the house at devilish hours of the morning and, clambering with red-eyed energy into his vehicle du jour, been whisked at speeds made more appalling by the twenty-four foot boat at their backs down to Delacroix Island. Hours later, ice chest stacked with speckled trout in their slender iridescence and pumpkin-bright redfish, they had returned in the cool of evening, skin sore with sun and slick with the oil the boat's big engine had pressed from their pores.

Memory clamored as the boys and Eloise now trudged up the straight front walk. The doorknob, gleaming in the Sun, scalded Roman's unsuspecting hand, but the foyer within was cool and dim. Eloise had never been there, for though she tolerated Simon and laughed loudly, if against her will, at his heavy-handed comedy, she considered him something of a pagan, as in fact he was, and reserved the right to keep clear of his influence. She peered about now, in vain, for crucifix or sacred visage, yet the immaculate surfaces and soaring ceilings soothed her hotel-harried sensibilities. Looking through the wide windows into the backyard, they spied Jack, gloved and masked, attempting to clean what he had salvaged on his return to their house that morning. All about him stood buckets, some of water, others of various cleaning solutions, into which he dipped the salvaged china and beer steins before scouring them with a soft toothbrush. Presently he noticed his wife and children and joined them within, Eloise recoiling slightly at the faint stench of flood. Thus they first met that odor, and even at a dilute remove it paid exorbitant tribute to the wreckage which had birthed it.

iii

Two days later, in the driveway of St. James's high school in Metairie, Roman and Francis met once again, gladly but not without some hesitation. Each was relieved that the other had returned, but each now realized how tenuous his hold on the other was. A new caution had entered their friendship; holds tightened and defenses were raised. They sat in the afternoon sun, cooling slightly with the first week of October, and related briefly their adventures of the intervening weeks.

"What was public school like?" Roman asked, with perhaps a touch of derision.

Francis studied his face. "I don't know. It was school. Different from here, that's for sure. One time I walked into the bathroom and people were on the floor doing it like dogs."

Roman's pupils widened as if to admit the images that now played behind them.

"What'd they do?"

"Just kept at it."

He felt now a twinge of some jealousy, at what he could not precisely have said.

Francis hurried on, "It wasn't all like that. Mostly they were just nice." He thought for a moment. "Remember that kid I told you about on the phone, the one with the Viagra shirt?"

"Mhm."

"Well, I got to know him--Jake was his name--not very well, but better than you'd think. He was the nicest. When I left, he gave me these to remember him by."

Francis extended his right wrist, to which clung two bracelets, apparently of rubber, red and black and barbed as wire.

Roman felt an odd tightening at his throat. "I'm really glad you came back," he said.

"Yeah, I wasn't going to, but then my dad said you were coming."

Over Francis's shoulder Roman had watched Fr. Muller strolling toward them as they talked, his high shoulders slightly hunched, his gait marked by a slight bounce, as though he were eternally aware of the atmospheric pillar he upheld. Francis, noticing Roman's gaze, turned half around, squinting into the sunlight slanting through an oak over Muller's shoulder.

"Good afternoon, gentlemen. How are we doing?"

"Ok, Father, how about you?"

"Jussst perfect." It was a common expression of his and a key facet of his fundamental irony. "Any progress on either of your homes?" He had an excellent memory and knew that both hailed from Lakeview.

"My parents haven't been back yet," said Francis.

"My dad's gutting ours."

"He grew up in Lakeview, is that right?"

"That's right—oh! and he found something when he first went back. My mom taped a Divine Mercy card to the door before we left, and when Dad got there, the image was gone but the words 'Jesus I trust in you' were still stuck to the door. It wasn't even taped at the bottom. The flood just sort of plastered it there."

"I guess that's about as good a sign as you could ask for," Francis offered with what struck Roman, glancing toward his friend, as a kind of forced politeness.

Fr. Muller merely smiled slightly, an odd smile somehow articulated by turning down the corners of his mouth.

"Very good, gentleman. Good luck this evening," and he hunched away once again. Over his shoulder he said, "Mr. Higgins, kindly remove your shackles."

With a hard stare at the retreating back Francis slid the bands from his wrist and slipped them into the outermost pocket of his backpack.

iv

While others wasted words, Spencer Zazulak had seated himself once again in a fresh stall. He was essentially fastidious and could not abide working anywhere where urine or worse could cloud his judgment, but he had followed contemporary art and knew that it led where art was not, to feces on canvas and glass houses in Times Square.

He remained unfazed at having left behind his Odyssey after just three weeks' work. He rejoiced at least to have left a mark where flood should not reach, and he took an ironic delight in the work's brevity.

Here he began anew. It was a Poundian dictum, after all, which had long ago selected his studio for him.

The Return of the Native

Houston couldn't stop
this slop that I drop,
and concrete can't starve
these lyrics I carve
from wicked Tex Mex
and Mexican sex,
so the verse has returned
though the pages have burned.

The opening door shook him from his ecstasy, and he hurriedly rose, flushed with the toe of his shoe, and stepped out, shaking his head at nature's demands, so insatiable in their lust after art.

v

That day, too, Roman and Francis met Ruggieri again. His class fell just before dinner. The mood throughout the afternoon had been festive, relations between teachers and students familiar. The ebullient fraternity of tragedy leavened the school community in those months, enfolding all but the most misanthropic of its members, and after a valiant effort to lecture on the Scopes trial, Ruggi was derailed, not quite unwillingly. Lifelong New Orleanian, he far preferred words to work.

The boys' means today lay in questions of sexual ethics, pertinent enough to bear justification, tantalizing enough to bear attention.

"Ruggi, is it a sin to beat your meat?" a thin, tan, weasel-faced yet obviously innocent boy asked.

Roman snapped to attention. He had to this point passed the class by imagining Ruggi with a mustache. He had long ago realized how easily his mind's eye applied whiskers to any man's face (try as he might, he could never master the trick with women). The diversion's only downside was its permanence. Once envisioned, the altered face could be razed only with great difficulty.

"Why do you guys always have to stir up ----? Why?!"
"Because we're ---- stirrers, Ruggi!" he responded in mock antiphon.

"Seriously, is it a sin?"

"The Church says yes; Ruggi says no. No good lettin' stuff build up like that."

"Ok, good, because I always feel weird going to confession and telling the priest I beat my meat."

Twenty-five brains blazed with license. A multitude of tinglings commenced.

"How far is too far?"

"Let me ask you something—let's say Bobby over here takes a Loyola co-ed out, and later on they get hot and heavy—to the point...of orgasm—is she still a virgin?" His speech rolled on with an expert sense of the dramatic, his voice at all times exactly modulated to the wedding of sense and sound.

Thus passed forty-five minutes which left every boy in the room aroused, some to a feverish anxiety to reach the restroom, others, who lived through school in a state of utter torpor, to a mere wakefulness.

For his part, Roman felt as though a dialogue which had gone on quietly for years within his mind had been brought to the fore. Thought, swollen to indistinction with act, rushed through him with cruel pleasure.

He and Francis said nothing of the class over dinner, each somehow apprehensive as to what the other might say. Both slept that night with a sense of relief. They had at last finished the first day of school, and in its passing new concessions had been tendered.

vi

The neighborhood Roman grew up in has since become one of the most fashionable and expensive of New Orleans' various boroughs, popular especially among conservative young professionals determined to raise their children in safety in the city that raised them and their parents and grandparents and so on evidently back to Adam who of course was formed on the East Bank of the Mississippi. At the time of our story, though, Lakeview was known for its quaint cottages and quiet ranks of elderly tenants. Before that it was a territory in dispute, a chiefly familial province into which the grisly conflicts of narcotics occasionally spilled. Roman's earliest memories of home (so early that he could never ascertain whether they were memories in the true sense or fabrications founded on photographs) featured the lot's prior occupant, dark beneath dark skies and cluttered with gnarled crepe myrtles. Just as the new home's mild yellow paint had been applied, Roman's father, jogging about the neighborhood, had discovered a body stashed in an azalea bed three blocks away. They had nearly moved immediately, and for years afterward Roman, accompanying his father on walks about the block, had taken the German Shepherd and the pocketed Ruger for granted.

Roman returned to this house for the first time nearly three weeks after the flood subsided. His father, of course, had inspected the damage a week earlier and determined how much might be salvaged, a limited list consisting mainly of some drums stacked atop a bunk bed, Eloise's china and ironic stein collection which, though moldy, might be cleaned, and the various photographic and taxidermic memorabilia hung sufficiently high to escape the storm's reach.

The light was grey the day Roman returned, and to a height of eight feet above the street all was grey as well. The flood, like a great dirty beast obsessively caressing every edge it met, had left the indelible line of its passage on every wall and trunk. Many of the trees had fallen; many had died and stood waiting to be torn up and burned.

In September's swift bakery the damp world had molded. All manner of modern wrack paved the streets: paper of every shade and stock reduced to grey pulp; dolls, paintings, photographs, all with faces forever effaced; kayaks, sailboats, yachts, boats of all description overmastered by their element and cast from their proud chromatic pageant into the ghastly Parmenidean plenitude of the mold which, unmoving, raised to itself the incense of the starkest stench Roman would meet. It was not the worst smell he had known. Public (even private) toilet, bag of bad meat, vomit, all could outclass it in intensity, but none shared its capacity to mold mind and memory. It hung everywhere, modulated to the tastes of homeowners, tinged with some perfume or the odor of leather furniture. It was the smell of human community stripped by the sea of the impoverished agency preserving it against rot.

Almost no one moved in the streets that day. A National Guard truck trundled occasionally up and down the blocks, long cracked and potted with the softness of the land and the explorations of the oak roots, checking in on the few ashen men moving through the molding air carting loads of sheetrock and swollen books and blackened furniture out to the street. In the coming weeks dump trucks would begin to haul away and pile the refuse on the grounds of a park situated in Lakeview's West End. Higher and higher loomed the putrid mound, higher than any building in the neighborhood. Today the park is green again with sapling cypress and maple, their youth yet a reminder.

The sun was still low--indeed, it would not show its face at all that day--as the Morans, Eloise excepted, turned onto their old street and nosed with utmost caution down its wrecked length. Roman peered as they crossed Francis's street toward the blue house which despite its distance appeared to his familiar eye as though just before him. He was relieved to find it intact, though the two magnolias in the front yard had fallen.

Presently they pulled to the curb before their home and stepped into the warm air, where they stood for some moments in awed contemplation of the fallen holly trees and cypress and the brown belt of the floodwater, sickly against the yellow underlying paint. Then they took the short, curved walk and the three stairs of brick, and the air cooled slightly as Roman stepped into his old home again. The cherry floors, not five years old, licked stickily at his soles. In places the boards had warped and coursed in treacherous ridges through the debris. Here and there shards of glass shaken from fallen picture frames, indistinguishable in the gloom from the dirty floors, sounded their further dissolution at his step. His breath grew hot and wet behind his mask, whose plastic scent mingled with the mildew and mold and brine.

His eyes struggled to form any sensible impression of the mess, of the green couch, the piano, the books and photographs, the music box he'd once buried in the back yard, the new curtains, the fresh wallpaper in the dining room, the china cabinet. So familiar in the framework of his day, they now swelled together, irretrievable in their diluvian solution.

Hesitantly he shuffled down the dark hall toward his bedroom. He nudged the door open with his foot and passed within, treading on the trunk of a stuffed elephant he had caught years before at a parade and which the flood waters had contrived to tip from his closet. Its plush hide had hardened. Through the one raised blind the white light of the morning shone as fresh as it ever had. The other, stuck shut from five years' abuses, hung brown and vivid and limp with mold as the same soft light spilled around its edges. The swamp mural surrounding his bed seemed to have taken on life for a moment only to fall extinct again with just a tortured variant of the swamp's scent remaining. The pair of mounted redfish, which had hung as if on a tree in the forefront of the scene, now lay on the floor, their tails cracked at the bases. A bluegill, caught in the spawn just before his eighth birthday, the worst piece of taxidermy he had met, hung on the opposite wall beside a pale blue cross, memento of his first communion. They stood out, strangely immaculate, against the white wall in its moldy arabesques.

He felt that the moment ought to bear some vast significance. He felt at least that he ought to feel more, that there was some rite he ought to perform. Instead he lifted a sheaf of paper jutting from the top shelf of his closet like the corner of a Caravaggian coffin. It was a book of animals he and Michael had drawn from encyclopedia pictures. He flipped the pages, enthralled by their whiteness. Here and there an image stood out to him, though most of all he remembered the amazement of that Saturday when, as page on page dispersed beneath their pencils, the lines at last took on some semblance to their inspirations. They had not drawn well, and it was just this that had amazed him, the inability of his hand to follow his eye or of his eye to follow the lines or of his mind to coordinate all three. Images of images eluded them.

"Come on, bud, let's get going. Mom won't want y'all in here long." His father stood in the doorway, looking around the room, picturing the days of gutting and renovation, and then turning slowly back down the dark hall. Roman followed after a moment. The corner of his desk scraped his thigh, leaving a dark streak on his jeans. His mother would wash them later, but the streak again, again would refuse to rise from the fabric until at last, years later, the jeans were thrown away.

Outside, where the brown and brittle trees lay on the drowned grass, Jack turned to the frame of the swing he'd once built to welcome his wife home from the hospital. The chains swung loose, and now over them he let fall a white sheet. On it he had written in large capitals, "LAKEVIEW, COME BACK."

They left the house then and wound through the strewn streets toward the center of the neighborhood, where they pulled into the asphalt yard of the parish church and its school. A Red Cross truck kept quiet watch there through the day, serving hot meals to those venturing irregularly into the neighborhood. It was there, perhaps by reference to the truck engine humming in the middle of the barren blacktop, that Roman first acknowledged the vast silence which had begun to press upon him in their house and which rolled in tremendous waves from the surrounding empty streets. They would come soon, but even the rats, it seemed, had not recovered from the flood.

Jack and Michael and Roman collected trays of beef stew and rolls from the window of the Red Cross truck and sat at a table with one other man, heavy-set, middle-aged, with dark eyes below bushy brows and a beige ball cap whitened with sweat. His jaws worked in obscurity behind his tangled black and white beard. From the hidden tongue Roman heard the sound of his father's name pronounced.

His father started slightly at the voice. "That you, Mark?"

"Yup. Been since we were here, huh?" He gestured toward the cafeteria.

"Think so. Whatcha up to?"

"Contractin, tryin to get in early, ya know. Ya brothers and sisters comin back?"

"Ahh, I'm sure they will."

"Send 'em my way if they do, huh?"

"Sure, sure. Hey, you need any guys?"

"Thought you's with the government?"

"They wanted me to move."

"Damn." He chuckled as he pondered this. "Well sure, I can use ya. Pay ain't commiserate with ya experience. They'll be lots a jobs though."

"What are you hearin?"

"You know, takes a damn act a God to get us kinda folks movin. Place is in the blood though. They'll be back. Gotta let it ovulate, ya know?"

Roman, emptying a packet of pepper into his dish, studied the man's face more intently. He had noticed that in each instance the man's eyes had widened and his hands described inestimable arcs, as though to highlight his malapropic jest. Then, as the dark eyes swung to meet his own, he dropped his gaze once again to his food. The reek of the streets mingled with each mouthful, but he chewed and swallowed in mechanical rhythm. The thought had not occurred to him that the neighborhood might not come back, at least not for many years. He knew his father would rebuild as soon as possible, even in spite of the bleak and perhaps perilous prospect of having the one clean new home in blocks of buildings lying abandoned, breeding mold and vermin and whatever else would throng to inhabit the languorous rot.

He wondered then if the rest of his family would come back. His grandmother, two aunts, one uncle, and six cousins all lived in the neighborhood. His other grandmother, not quite within the neighborhood, lived just two miles distant. As he considered the chance of their absence this first time, the memory arose of one October day two years before when, having come home from school and played football in the alley beside the house in the air just turning cold, he had felt, in a rush of feeling which now in the remembrance shriveled his bowels, that there could be no better neighborhood. Further again memory retreated to when he had told his father, feeling he must tell it however frightful it might be, that when he and his mother had died he, Roman, would buy the house. He sensed for once his love's contingency. He did not know that it would or could exist without the faces of his blood passing in the evenings as he and his father sat out in the garden warmed by hibiscus and honeysuckle and the Indian bottlebrush. He did not know if his love would remain were Grandma or Francis to go, and his father's present conversation with the man across the table, continuing in characters existent only in possibility, silenced him in his eating.

vii

On leaving the schoolyard twenty minutes later they drove two blocks toward the lake for the morning's last errand. They had decided to search Grandma Moran's house once more for any salvageable items Uncle Terry or Aunt Sarah might have missed in their earlier explorations. In particular, they wished to find some token to cheer her, something she might keep in her room in the Carmelite convent across the lake where she had taken refuge on returning from Lafayette.

It was one of Uncle Joe's creations, a wooden rocking horse he had crafted in honor of Roman's birth, that the latter most wanted to find when he, Michael, and his father arrived that September day for what would be their final visit to the family seat before its demolition. They approached the house, as usual, by the back door, passing by the iron gate that creaked in the same places as ever through the now grey garden stripped of its perennial redolence. One of the pecan trees had fallen across the yard and in its grey branches clung three squirrel nests, still and silent. As they entered the house, Roman was struck by the scent of the flood once more, here embattled by the laundry detergent which had spilled in the flood and spread across the room whose utter disarray mocked its desperate chemical attempts at cleanliness.

Turning into the dim downstairs den, Roman found the horse after a second's survey. Knocked at the hooves from its rocking rails but largely sound, surrounded by sodden books in moldering piles, it gazed up at him, its glass eye steady as ever, its fluent curves, by some strange calculus, yet urging him to clemency. Gingerly, trying to touch as little as possible even with their precautionary gloves, he and Michael lifted the two pieces, bore them outside, and laid them gently in the bed of the truck.

Jack had meanwhile picked his way around the house, once more to gather up the scenery of the final brief act. He passed the reliquary record player, the toppled china cabinet, the now dead grandfather clock; he slipped cleanly as he could down the hidden narrow hallway where he'd pretended to camp as a young, white-haired boy, lighting matches on the floor. He walked through the kitchen, his own moldy prints indiscernible against the linoleum, maculate for the first time in decades. The grey light of the day spilled equivocally across the countertops and tables, revealing in its purity the builders' fallible art. He had ceased years before to notice the smell of the house, and now, set against the slowly growing wreckage, it appeared to him once more, perhaps more memory than sensation.

The boys had rejoined him within and together they took from the stairway wall a large framed photograph of the beach outside the family house on Bay St. Louis. It was the photograph, hanging in the center of that house, that centered its memory in Roman's mind, leading his thought toward the vanishing point somewhere over the sea. As Michael and his father lifted the frame from the wall and carried it from the house, careful not to brush it against any of the lower, mold-soaked walls, he lingered a moment over the bare wall behind it traced in gentle fingers of rot. Then he left the house for the last time. Six weeks later it was demolished.

viii

The following day was bright, and as the Morans crossed the Causeway to Mandeville, Roman's mind ran before them, over the brown waves and then east through a forest of dense pines, thin and straight and mostly young, to the small city of Lacombe, its air thickened with woodsmoke, swamp, or sea; its bait shops shoulder to shoulder with Provencal restaurants; and its stately mansions overgrown with mobile homes and crumbling cottages heaped year on year with refuse, the grass yellowing and dying in the rusting shade of ancient chassis.

He thought, too, of the Carmelite convent toward which they thundered over the concrete joints, of its forty forested acres nestled in a bend of Bayou Lacombe. And he thought of its long life, known to him not in any detail but in the tremulous history woven of unlooked for images cascading from the parents' endless musings after meals: images of sisters once abundant and blooming, praying in the long college on the hill; catching catfish in the farm pond and stripping their dull silver skin at a post set at the pond's edge; planting rose gardens, tending azaleas, burying their dead in a small plot above the bayou. There came to mind the cement tubs scattered over the property, and from them swelled the cold, holy idyll of wet limbs, white with habit, rising like swans' necks into the pure air.

And then his own brief part in the pageant: dawn romps in the mist in quest of geese, brief races to the water's edge, the thrown stick fast in white feathers; stubby fingers' strife with fine line, the endless vanishing of cricket and cork and the miraculous emergence of the bluegill's painted cheek, the shiner's shallow drift and the landed cat flopping on the green bank; and more the endless circuit of the shore, the stern course in casting and the vain lust for bass breaking the surface's silence with the red rattle of their crisp gills and the harlotry of chance. And the precipitous certainty of proximity.

And the distant vision of Aunt Sarah, coming counter to his orbit, crying out for first news from afar. Or her apparition at his back and his turning from sunset over the pond into the plangent declamation: "It is a beauteous evening, calm and free."

For a moment Roman was shaken from his reverie by a growing need to urinate, aggravated by the car's rhythmic bouncing over the bridge. He focused again on the waves, the long low swells dotted white with gulls. And he turned to the photograph with him in the back seat, its view, over low dunes dotted in cane bent lightly in a low breeze, of Bay St. Louis under a grey sky. Piers grey with age, many stripped to pilings, stepped into the waves' waist-deep surging. Gulls hung high in the wind, their eyelids low. And he was there now as well, with the slow highway at his back and behind it the Carmelite villa with its disproportion of bedrooms and its dull green floor forever flecked with sand that rasped beneath the Morans' bare feet in their summer pilgrimage. With his band of cousins he lay in the hot afternoon shallows or raced down the wet desert strip, watchful against the hardhead cats sticky in the sun and stiff with death, shouting when in the clear of low tide there shown a stingray's ghostly hull, while the parents basked beneath umbrellas. And followed evening feasts of fish and crabs and shrimp at long plastic tables laden in the shade of the oaks plodding to the sand. And the final rite of Grandma's descent from porch to pine path to sand and out far, far on the dusk's bare ribbons of bar and into the troughs never deeper than her ankles and cool already with the light's lifting toward the stars.

Roman's musings scattered on the car's descent to shore and the forest's sudden flux. Soon Jack turned onto the small country highway that led to the Carmelite property, and Roman asked if he might be the bearer of the photograph. They had come to Lacombe that day to celebrate Grandma's birthday, and though they should perhaps have gathered there under ordinary circumstances, the college had become most eminently suitable by the fact of Aunt Sarah's having installed Grandma in one of its vacant rooms. (A few others, mostly old women but also one young family with a large golden retriever--its head presently consigned to a cone in token of recent fits of anxious scratching--had taken up a genteel refugee existence there. For once the scarcity of vocations gave cause for thanks.)

Though Lacombe lay nearer New Orleans, the family heart burned always for the scene in the photograph, and Roman silently believed himself most faithful of them all to its love. He had often lingered there long after the rest had reverted to the city, rising at dawn to join Aunt Sarah on the screened porch, quiet with the early sea. It was then, while they waited for Grandma to wake, which she invariably did not until mid-morning had passed, that he learned of poetry, Sarah reciting lines and lines of Yeats and Hopkins while he sat enraptured less by sense (his mind scarcely sorted the words as they passed him and dispersed on the moist air) than sound, her voice swelling, ecstatic with emotion regulated by the rhythm of the sea.

So it was with rather a proprietary sense that, himself mostly obscured by its large frame, Roman bore the photograph down the convent's long hall, scented of chocolate cake, to the mass of his family in the foyer, and he felt their easy excitement swell in the sudden clamor which itself served as chorus to the Bay's music.

Grandma looked at the picture for a moment in the hall, smiling with a light which seemed to spread from some treasury of herself. She looked at Roman, peering over the top of the frame to see her reaction, and said, "Oh, Roman, it's beautiful." She had seen it ten thousand times and still she seemed now to see it for the first. And he in turn had seen the look she wore now each afternoon at the Bay, when they sat again on the porch and she pointed out the whitecaps whipped up in the invariant two o'clock breeze.

Aunt Sarah took the picture then and carried it to Grandma's room, where she hung it and stepped back amid expressions of admiration. The Morans were a simple people and easily satisfied, and they moved together to the chapel then, attended by a small host of sisters and a priest they'd summoned to celebrate a birthday Mass for Grandma. These family Masses, foreign to Roman's liturgically conservative experience in their proneness to the odd strain of dance or secular song, had always by their strangeness pressed a measure of comfort into Roman's prayers. Today, for instance, in place of a sermon Aunt Sarah delivered an encomium in Grandma's honor. When she attempted to open the floor, Uncle Joe, never very homiletically patient, moaned and waved his hands and said, "Come on, let's keep this show rollin!" Most laughed, Roman not excepted. Few of them were particularly pious, few even regular churchgoers, yet Roman sensed in those Masses a kind of perfection to their grand collective impatience. It was, in light of this last, a brief service, and shortly they adjourned to the convent cafeteria for lunch. Roman talked to Uncle Joe as they waited in line for roast beef and rice and gravy.

"How do you think the Saints'll do this year, Uncle Joe?"

"Ahhhh they'll probably be terrible again."

"You don't think the offense'll keep it together?"

"Nope." They laughed together in grim conspiracy. Decades of loss had plunged the city into athletic pessimism, the indulgence of which was one of its greatest comforts.

"Any word from Mr. George?"

"That idiot stayed in his house," here Joe began to wave his short fists in small circles, head-high. "Coast Guard had to come get his crazy ass off the roof."

As in like manner all about the family ate and talked, dispersed and coalesced in laughter, stories, exchanges of news over the broad network of their mutual acquaintance, the pond down the hill began by its distant glance to exercise its solitary temptation. Though he sensed that to fish that day would constitute a mild indiscretion, Roman had that morning, while his parents showered and dressed, slipped a small pole into the back seat of the car. Now he pocketed a roll, passed back into the main hall, and gained again the outside air, quiet but for the drum of woodpeckers. Taking his pole and casually concealing it behind his frame, he followed the white stone path to the water.

He stepped into a clear space among cattails at the pond's edge, plucked a bit of bread from his pocket, and, rolling it tight, pierced it with the small hook, which he cast to the far corner of a grey pier some twenty feet from shore. The cork settled and after a few seconds began gently to bob. An image appeared to Roman of large eyes set in an oval iridescence. Soon the cork shot down into the dark water; rapidly raising the tip of the rod he was vexed to see the cork return to the surface. He found his hook bare; quickly affixing a fresh ball of dough, he returned it to its place. Just as the cork began again to tremble, he felt a soft, cold pressure on his shoulder and, startled, whirled as though guilty to a pair of round eyes, cobalt and electric. Aunt Sarah resolved slowly out of the field of their pulsation.

"Thank you for doing that for Grandma," she said.

Recovering quickly, finding himself uncharged, he smiled. "I'm glad she's looking so good."

"Yes, I think she gets prettier every year, don't you?"

Roman had never considered this, and its contrariety at first puzzled him. Grandma had been in his earliest memories fat, doughy, her coal eyes clapped into her face, the model for his later imaginings of Faulkner's Miss Emily. Since then she'd grown slimmer, gained color. Her smile was her readiest expression, and none of the coarseness and vitriol which might naturally arise in a woman widowed young and grown slowly old had surfaced in her.

He had turned back to his cork as he thought, and, seeing it motionless, retrieved it. The bread was gone. "How is she doing?" he asked as he turned back and the two began a slow progress around the pond.

"Well, you know, '*It's just so still here*'," she imitated her mother's constant complaint against Lacombe. Then, her smile fading as her eyes wrinkled at the corners in concern, she said in a quieter voice, "But I think she's doing well."

Their gentle pace brought them now to the fountain at the North end of the pond, a timed spectacle which rose and fell by the hour, recycling the pond's water in a small elevated pool which, overflowing, cascaded down a small stone dam into the main body. At the center of a bridge level with the dam they paused and leaned against the rail. The fountain's mist breathed on the backs of their necks as they looked out over the water. Plastic worms and crankbaits hung on a wire overhead, reminders to cast well if only for fear of looking foolish. On the opposite bank romped several children and the golden retriever in the presence of a stout figure Roman now recognized as the Carmelite from the hotel in St. Francisville.

"It is still."

He cast toward the stump of a cypress.

"Sometimes. But other times the wind on the pond is just perfect. I don't think it's so much the stillness that gets Grandma as the scope of the place. But once she's got her word…"

He popped the cork gently. Nothing.

"Have you been to the Bay?"

"Nothing but slabs up and down the beach. I went last Tuesday."

"Did you find anything at the house?"

"Just that blue cat from the bathroom," and she began to laugh, a high, wheezing laugh, startling to the uninitiate and infectious to the family. The object in question, a plastic feline of dull hue and dubious purpose, had after years of attempts at more honorable employment been at last relegated to the beach house bathroom, where it kept fading eye affixed on the doors of the three stalls.

"That thing scared me so much when I was little."

"There's providence for you. It was under the oak out back." She paused, frowned, continued, "The pines and the pier are gone, but other than that the land's the same."

"All of them gone?"

"No pines left. And just a few of the pier's pilings."

"Will y'all be able to rebuild any time soon?"

"Eventually. Once we get the insurance money and agree on a new plan."

"I miss it more than my house."

Roman would miss the house, though it could not have been itself without the pines out front, and he would miss the pines, too, though his feet would not. The walk from the house to the beach had always been the harshest part of the brief life at the Bay, the passage over the needles and seeds and the heat of the beach highway and the sand itself flecked with oyster shells. But he would miss the pines and their scent, wafting heavily about the swing in their shade.

Roman followed the progress of a turtle toward the stump and his cork; nervous, he retrieved it again. He felt, meanwhile, her eyes on him, burning blue, absent any customary hesitation.

"And how is Francis?"

She had inherited her mother's mode of "and" and sharpened its power of solicitude.

"I don't know." He cast toward another stump. "Different."

"How?"

"I can't really tell. It's almost like he's become more a part of himself, or like a little part of him took over." His cork had darted downward, but again he missed.

"What does that mean?"

"I don't know." He cast anew, whipping the rod this time. Then, abruptly, "I'm afraid he doesn't believe in God anymore."

She could not suppress a slight smile. "I remember once when you all were fishing here and he managed to swing a perch up over the telephone wire." Roman smiled, too, at the image of the two-handed hookset and the brief bow in the cane pole and the bluegill rocketing from the dark. She continued, "Did he ever believe in God?"

This stunned him. "Well, I thought so. He knows more about God than I do."

He again felt her gaze, pitying yet unperturbed. "I wouldn't worry too much. Nothing more normal than doubt, especially at this age."

They grew silent again as the cicadas took up their roar in a moss-draped oak leaning over the water. A water moccasin slid from the warm stones on the bank as a pileated woodpecker raked his chuckling flame through the pines above their heads.

She looked at him again, the blue eyes like his father's but more piercing, as if more used to sights both very near and very far. He looked at her, glanced away, saw the turtle resurface near his cork, looked at her again. He retrieved his line and began to walk, descending from the bridge and shadowing the line of azaleas along the pond toward Aunt Sarah's house, a white two-story just above the bayou ringed in roses and Live Oaks.

"Maybe they washed out in the flood?" she asked, indicating the pond's dark surface.

"No, they're in there. Just keep missing 'em." Then, after several steps, his long for his height and slow, hers swift and purposive, "Can I ask you about something else, Aunt Sarah?"

"Yes."

He wondered for a moment how best to put it. Half his family were teachers and to doubt one was foreign.

"I don't really trust our Scripture teacher."

"Hm."

"I mean, his class is great. But he's always telling us to question everything."

"Ah." She began to see. "Well, it's not how I'd run a class, but aren't you all questioning everything anyway?" she asked, laughing lightly.

"Not me."

"Well, not with your parents, no."

Her levity began to grate. "But what am I supposed to do?"

"Do you need to do anything?"

"I keep feeling like I should."

"If you want my advice, pray for your class and be Francis's friend."

They were strolling upstream along the bayou then, the movement of its brown water imperceptible except by the occasional fallen leaf or insect which floated along awaiting the flooding of its cells or the blind strike of a bluegill or bass.

He hadn't looked for this discussion but the hope he'd felt in its commencement had departed.

She stopped and, turning, asked, "Why do you want Francis to believe?"

The question seemed to him absurd. He stumbled over his answer, embarrassed. "So we...so I don't..."

"What I want to know is whether this is more about him or about you?"

A feeling as of fraud crept over him. They had circled Aunt Sarah's house and stood now between it and the sisters' swimming pool, breathing the bloom of Angel Trumpet.

"Even Mary had a question. Just think about that. But don't think too much, because this isn't a problem for you to solve."

She sensed he would say nothing more then, so they turned and walked back up the hill to the convent, twenty-three feet above the Bayou. As they approached, the faces of their family appeared through the glare on the large windows of the dining hall, and laughter above all else spoke silently through the panes. Nearly all of them--Grandma, Uncle Joe, Uncle Terry, Aunt Ruth, all their children--had been displaced, and all of them laughed, reassured in their mutual insecurity that all at least would be complete even if completely changed.

Roman would later draw some solace from Aunt Sarah's advice, but his sullen presence, inflamed somewhat by the reddening dampness spreading beneath his jeans, was greeted on his re-entry to the general festivities by a typical sally from his Uncle Terry.

"What's up, Rome, ya big fruit? Gonna join up? Been gettin' fitted for a habit?" He smiled broadly, his red face folding in along its habitual lines.

"No bigger fruit around than you, Uncle T," Michael rejoined on his brother's behalf, jabbing Terry in his bulging gut.

The red face reddened further as he smiled still more broadly at Michael. He saw in the skinny little boy a kindred spirit deserving the most spirited attacks.

"Don't get me started on you, ya little retard. I'll knock ya ugly little face in."

"Yeah, yeah, ya fat fool!"

The party continued in like manner for two hours more. For a time the pall of his musing veiled Roman's sense, yet before long he was drawn out into the efflorescent spectacle of his blood: his aunts chattering, laughing sharply in the low New Orleans manner; his uncles discussing work, the Saints, the storm-mad mayor; Grandma Moran smiling, benign co-creatrix, across whatever barren expanse, of all the life she saw.

IV.

OVERMUCH IN THE SUN

And the second decade dawned, morning slowly with sudden summer and shorts still slightly damp with urine sharp against his nose and cold, trailing its quickly lifting film as he and his brother lingered on the hardwood floor, blind in holiday to her as half-shod she limped into the living room and strained said, "Where's Dad," and slouched back down the hall.

Then time to change had passed when the father flashing through the den shouted 'now now now' so that before the third he leapt leaving the last wide disc to dissipate. Down through the banks of bloomed azaleas in June's cool humors and into the car and then the dim room waiting in the yellow lamps with potted plants slinging lingering vines down along the backs of the chairs and all through his shorts then briefs drying and dry though the yellow scent clung and harried as they sat silent and alone. Now shifting stiffly in the leather car, the uncle's blonde lick flashing in the front seat and they laughing at the red shock of soda so early. And through the day games despite his father saying somewhere in the afternoon decadent with misted glass that "Yes, she could die," and the possible now known yet not believed. And still the yellow scent if only to him.

And neither of them then, not until their third decade's decline, had heard of her lying in the white scanner, about to seize, speechless, near deaf but for the doctor confessing, "She will not last the night, no, so pray." And still unable when the bishop appeared with oil, body, and stole for comfort against the sightless black wings beating out an Erinyetic justice as she wept at the tongue corrupted for contrition and the mitred voice mute of every light urging, "I will answer, I will answer, I will answer, do not be afraid."

And all was done for comfort and more for delight: the games beside the sea, the smoke of charcoal, rich fat of beef dripping and swift slip of card across levee with sudden red of white skin tumbling over grass, cartoons returning out of his father's fatherless memory as the three slept in one bed of his father's unfolding fear framed by four posts patterned after vines and cones.

And then as they said to his speechlessness there came the Jesuit with the bit of bone, double relic of Seelos and the first Jesuit, now dead, who had wed and baptized and eaten in their house smiling stroking the collie to the piano's chatter. And they bought a golden chain and draped the bone about her neck as she had passed beyond the night and still the right, the arm leg cheek lay dead and the doctor said she would not and would not play the piano again though now at least she could speak and said "Miss-is-sip-pi Ri-ver Bridge" again, again at their commands as to an infant, clapping, clapping for the shivering tongue.

Then on the fifteenth day as the Mass moved unblinking on the screen there came the final sign from habit and the arm rose as it had and the fingers flexed and she took the miniature keyboard and the 9th confined to two octaves rolled in electric legato from the resurrected fingers as her mother from the bathroom burst, "Eloise! Eloise! You're playing!"

And now again he had a mother and she sat every evening on the new swing with midsummer in the garden and untied rocked as sun flooded the swollen clouds above the lake and the bees began to soften in the bottlebrush. And again he had a mother and at last a father.

i

October passed as it must, and the weather, rarely very cold in New Orleans, took on a golden uniformity as if in gentle effort at amends. Classes continued, at last uninterrupted, and Roman slowly grew used to postulates and theorems, exegetic principles, and even declensions and conjugations (his new Latin teacher, a man of much experience, had dispensed with all emphasis on macrons). More importantly, perhaps, he found himself, not by any certain effort toward the end, part of a ring--a very small ring, and very far from the center, but a part nonetheless of the school's swirling centripety.

Slowly, too, a change stole over Francis. Essentially cheerful, he had however always nursed a sullen streak which passed now into disposition. Swearing, previously an occasional indulgence, now formed the fiber of much of his public conversation, and Roman, whether from his habit of imitation or his faint jealousy at the laughter Francis now drew from their customary dinner companions, slowly took up the thread.

Roman noticed, too, that Francis's anger seemed at once most and least active during Scripture class. He participated little, but as Ruggieri led them into Exodus, Roman, glancing toward Francis in conspiracy or turning to whisper some comment, found himself frequently taken aback by a dark, distant ardor in his friend's attention. Slowly he began to surmise--he would never inquire--that the kindling lay in

Ruggieri's basic exegetical technique, which was to provide each seemingly supernatural occurrence in Scripture with a rational (and almost universally natural) explanation. He demonstrated that each of the plagues, for instance, could be connected with known phenomena--locust migrations, dinoflagellate tides in the Nile, sudden virulence. A ten-foot layer of clay deep in the fertile crescent's crust accounted for Noah's flood. The Red Sea was the Reed Sea. Prevailing winds, vegetable encrustations, vast idiot quail. All reasonable enough, and it was just in the reason that Roman didn't like it. Pugnacious in his quiet way, he resolved to confront the old man. Lingering over his books one day until his classmates had filed out for dinner, he finally sidled to the podium. Ruggieri, bent within a foot of a stack of essays, saw nothing of his approach, and Roman, suddenly repulsed by the spotted scalp, very nearly continued past in silence. At the last moment he turned and, swiftly but hesitantly, began: "Hey, Ruggi?"

The old man looked up at the first syllable, his blue eyes seeming to contract within his motionless lids. "Ah, Moran. What can I do for you? Glad you're not as much a goof off as your daddy."

Roman had thought to pose his problem bluntly, but now, offered the chance, he dallied. "Did you teach my dad?"

"Oh yeah, and your Uncle Terry and Mitch and, what was the other one's name? Mark?"

"Yes, sir."

"Yehp, buncha screwballs, same as now. Your daddy's changed the most."

Roman, who had never heard of Telemachus, had begun to chafe. "Why don't you treat the miracles like miracles?"

"Do you believe they're actually miraculous?" Ruggieri asked, not in the least fazed.

And Roman, very solemnly, "I do."

"You don't think it's a little over the top? I mean, come on, a whole river into blood."

And Roman, beginning to enjoy: "Yeah, exactly, that's the fun. If I was God I wouldn't go just using algae. Your way it's just like...like Ozymandias or some waste of time."

"Oh ho ho, look who's cracked a book." There was no malice in the mockery. "Well, look, first of all, I think you're right. And it's definitely a better story that way. Let me ask you this, though: do you think most of those guys sitting around you believe the miracles? Do you think the average guy walking down Bourbon thinks the Nile actually turned into blood?"

"I don't know. I want them to believe that. I know some people in here do."

"Yeah, sure, sure, some of them do. But for most of them it's *just* a story, not a story the way you're thinking of it. I'm looking out at a bunch of kids who are gonna be doctors and lawyers some day, and I want to prove to them that it's at least possible that everything in that book actually could have happened."

"But why does it matter if it happened if God didn't have anything to do with it?"

"You mean this way makes him into some kind of wizard of Oz?"

"Yeah, exactly."

"Well, did the wizard of Oz will the scarecrow to have a heart or the lion to be brave? Did his providence have anything to do with it?"

"Well, no."

"See, that's what I'm saying. My point isn't to say that these miracles didn't happen. My point is God willed it to happen, but he did it with the rules he'd built in already. He set the whole thing in motion back in Genesis. That way God doesn't violate his design by jumping in to interfere."

Thus God or nature.

Roman would perhaps have brooded long over this interchange were it not for a curious encounter on his subsequent way to dinner. He hurried down a long breezeway, despite himself admiring as he went a crepe myrtle, one of the few still in bloom, which had caught his attention by its rare bright red hue. Its crimson branches spread above a long, low storage shed set against the school's iron fence. As he neared the shed's end he became suddenly aware of hysterical laughter which he now realized had been rising for some time. Slowing his pace, he passed the shed and stood staring at a slight blond boy clinging to the fence, feet on the lowest rung, hands on the highest, eyes squinting and coruscant with sunlight slanting above the breezeway and directly into his face. His irises bore a blue brilliance which somehow by shade alone evidenced a long acquaintance with the jocund.

Beginning to laugh himself (his abiding fear of the insane notwithstanding), Roman hesitantly approached and asked the boy what he was doing. The suspended one replied through tears that, having laughed during class and, on interrogation, responded that he'd laughed at nothing, he'd been condemned to hang here during half of dinner, laughing at nothing. To Roman's stare he answered that while it had been terribly awkward at first he had come to see how perfectly funny the whole thing was.

So Roman walked on beneath the myrtles' dwindling pannicles, his meditations lightened slightly by a fresh salvo of laughter born, remotely at least, of a football coach in his unwitting contrapassic genius.

Such diversions were legion. To the young mind in its burgeoning brain they are necessary. Yet unlike them the vapor of heterodoxy did not then pass as the bracing breath of a stranger's cigarette but rather bound one band of daily experience as the odor of smoke in a hidden room long devoted to the purpose. Thus one day shortly after, in a brief aside to a discussion of the Canaanite tribes, Ruggieri sowed again his innocent discord.

"Alright, who can tell me what the Greek word *theos* means?"

"God," said the red-eyed Paul Lala, a wrestler who frequently roused himself from haggard slumbers to answer such etymological queries.

"Good. So a theist is someone who believes in God. A monotheist believes in one God, a polytheist multiple gods. An atheist doesn't believe in God. Can anyone tell me what the Greek word *gnosis* means now?"

Blank faces. Paul remained silent, though his matted locks yielded no clues as to whether mind or body had succumbed.

Ruggieri at length supplied the lack. "It comes from the Greek word meaning essentially 'knowledge,' especially knowledge of an arcane sort. That leads us to our last kind of person, the agnostic, someone who's not sure whether to believe God exists or not. Most of us are some kind of agnostic since we don't ever fully know God until the Beatific Vision, though the more we progress toward Sainthood, the more we will come to the kind of direct experience of God that gives knowledge."

Half an hour later class let out and the boys filed into the hall. The time had changed, and the Sun was well down now as all currents merged on courtyard and cafeteria. Roman trailed Francis, happily absorbed in pre-prandial reflection. With Roman occasions of sin lay never more distant than the next meal. His father had remonstrated with him frequently and with an almost total lack of consequence about the dangers of overeating. Once, for instance, when Roman had taken a particularly large second helping of jambalaya, his father had delivered what was initially intended as a brief warning and which evolved into a rather magnificent exordium on the virtues of health and continence. Roman, stolid in the face of beauty, had asked in response for someone to pass the salt.

The boys were in the cool night air between buildings now; the crowd about them thinned and disappeared as Roman wondered why Francis was walking so slowly. The latter, till then impassive, stopped suddenly in a breezeway, just at the point where two pools of light nearly met in a thin band of sharpened shadow. As they faced each other, light spreading on either side, Roman's bowels shriveled, seized suddenly by a fear which he recognized plainly when it came into the open.

"I think I'm an agnostic now."

Again, the feeling of responsibility, the thickening flush.

"Ok."

"It's just...what is he for? If all those miracles were just part of the way things usually are, what's the point of him? It's like you were asking Ruggi the other night."

Roman wondered that his friend had heard. "Yeah, well, like he said, there's gotta be something organizing it all. And it's not like Ruggi disproved every miracle that's ever happened. What about my mom?"

"Well...I know that's really important to you, but isn't it more likely that there was some natural explanation the doctors just didn't understand? Just like the Egyptians didn't know it was just algae in the Nile? Think about how much more we'll know in three thousand years, even a hundred. Anyway, no offense, but speaking of your mom, why isn't she happier? She thinks God did this thing for her, but what is she doing about it? I mean, my mom seems happier than yours."

"So?"

"Well, it's not like my mom believes in God."

Roman said nothing. His gaze, devolving to the concrete, began in embarrassment to trace the lines of light. Clara Higgins had seen that her sons went to Mass on Sundays, attended catechism classes, said their prayers at night. Perhaps it was for this that Roman had not noticed that she herself showed no belief. No crucifix hung above her bed, no miraculous medal about her neck; perhaps she had said grace before a dinner or two. Yet her life moved in evident rhythm, free from any outward disturbance save the sometime shade of road rage. Eloise Moran prayed unceasingly, a fact she took no pains to hide, yet her prayer seemed that of the hounded and bayed.

Francis continued, his voice trembling, sliding, it seemed, down into his throat. "And I keep thinking about the people in the attics."

Roman, unable somehow to hold his friend's eye, touched his shoulder. "I know," he said softly.

"I just keep seeing them up there. And I don't understand. Why would he save the Israelites, why would he save your mom, and still let them bake up there? All he had to do was stop the levee from breaking. No locusts, no paralysis. Just had to stick a toe down for a second." He again gathered himself. "You remember Gaspardi?"

Had Francis asked the question under circumstances different in the slightest, Roman should have laughed. Mr. Gaspardi, watching the boys at play in Francis's yard, had figured tragically in their earliest imaginings. An ill-shot basketball, passing over his solid white fence, either returned not at all or appeared punctured in the alley and after several weeks' passage. Slowly, of course, he had become a comic figure, and the boys did not conceal their laughter against his gaze.

Now, though, beginning to guess, he said nothing.

"I found him."

Roman's breathing deepened.

"My dad brought us to the house a while ago, and I was out on the court, and I looked up at his window and he was there. Like he'd never moved. And then I saw a rat."

In the light's dim interchange they stood silent some moments. Roman, afraid to vomit, looked away down the series of small fields between the buildings toward the quadrangle where their fellows sat in established groups, one student here or there picking his way among the seated toward a restroom or garbage can.

Across his tongue there raced a dozen arguments and comforts. Continually the thought occurred to him that his mother yet would die, that the Israelites all had died, that, yes, the point to him was that they all would die.

Perhaps his mouth began dumbly to work; perhaps Francis foresaw his thought or had himself turned to such reflections. At any rate he continued, "Look, I don't necessarily want to be convinced one way or another. I just wanted to tell you I'm not sure."

They walked off toward the quad then, Roman suddenly relieved. They resumed the discussion just twice, and then only for moments, in the next decade. Outwardly the mechanism of their friendship remained the same, but it became apparent, in a word here, a gesture there, a look of embarrassment, that a gulf had opened between them, infinitely deep but narrow enough that they might walk still hand in hand and hear each other clearly above a low and insistent grumbling.

ii

That night as blindly he lay whirling from the sun, unable to conjure sleep to his side on the blue leather couch, alternately staring at the high ceiling or wandering through unquiet regions of memory and bright sidereal shade unfolding behind his eyelids, he prayed. And as his urgency increased he felt more sharply his abstraction from the light. The sense of relief he had nursed through the earlier evening, consequent on fear's fresh definition, had disappeared. Cold, he decayed toward some core of frozen flame, and though he lay as a fallen corpse, his mind, like a bat thrown down from its gable, beat out desperate images. From a wood's chill night his friend, now stripped, now lashed, stumbled up desert ways distorted by bestial faces. Longing to offer some comfort he nonetheless grew hot with justice.

He rolled, shivered with sweat lifted from the breathless blue leather. A vague sickness began in his gut, as if, awakening at an odd night hour and wondering for some time at his sleeplessness he had realized he would before long vomit. It was the nascent waiting which had always tried him most and driven him, pressed shaking to the bed as though rolled in storm, to desperate prayer for passage. In the midst of his present pleading he dropped, as sometimes happened, too, in his sickness, into strange dreams. Now a great bearded man, deeply creased and reclining on a wrinkled blue couch, gazed into a blank and brilliant television screen, his hand in endless cycles from mouth to bowl of popcorn and back, his eyes fixed upon the screen's spectacular vacuity. The bulk of the yellow kernels broke between his ancient grey teeth, though some, slipping, lodged in his beard or settled amid the several folds of his voluminous belly, while now and then one in infinite descent ended its career beneath the couch where it lay decaying slowly to be borne away by rats, chattering and red-eyed and frightened.

Then he himself stood naked in a desert place, passing urine on the sand in what seemed a perfect solitude, but then appeared the bearded man, staring still, still seated on his couch in his ceaseless eating, now roaring laughter as he, again he, was dandled on the desert wind, hardening and trembling until the seed burst, pearl clumps arcing in the hard light to the sand which dried in seconds, and then from the golden ground erupted prickly pear, emerging full-grown to blossom in short-petalled yellow flowers which burst in white light.

He woke as November dawned, the grey light glimmering in rain that raced along the living room window, and his blue shorts, still slightly damp, were stiffening with faint white crust.

iii

By the time Roman awoke that day his mother had left the house. Had there been anyone to tell, she would have said that she was running errands. Her errands afforded her children no end of speculation, for she ran them often and at length and rarely returned with anything tangible. In their wildest weavings the boys had supposed her an intelligence operative of some sort, a fantasy which served not only to increase their admiration of her by some imaginative degrees but also to account for the stress she so often evidenced.

The reality was far more mundane and sacred. Her errant hours took her most frequently to one of the host of open chapels wherein she placed her refuge, principally from the myriad agencies which sought to inspire in her plans for her own salvation. An acute sense of her sin drove her often to an anguished adoration and a brief shriven ease.

Patriotism, both familial and national, dwelled deep in her consciousness. Consequently, it had taken her some years to see that in matters at least of sin effort corresponded little with success, or that if it did the effort was not principally hers. This revelation had driven her with increasing regularity to the confessional, wherein she maintained a relative ease on her own account.

In her husband and sons lay her heel, though, and Satan, playing Paris, twanged his darts thus swift and deep, and even as she knelt in the pedestrian chapel of a suburban church she was aware only of two fiery presences, the one an aquiline, monstrant burning before her, the other a gelid inflammation beneath. Again and again unbidden the image of her sons in the frigid teeth arose, and she begged that it should not be so, that she indeed should be swallowed instead or that at least she be allowed to speak what words were needed.

At length, opening her eyes on the altar, she rose and went in to her confession. She made it always face to face, as practice, she told herself, for whatever God's face should turn out to be; she made it without fuss or obfuscation; never had she sent a desperate friar in search of tissue. Presently she rose, but before she could go the priest said, "Excuse me, ma'am, but--I feel the need to ask--do you have sons?"

She said, her head turned slightly to one side, that she did.

After a moment's downward glance, he said, "I'm not sure why, but I feel called to tell you that your sons will do great things."

Heart especially eased, she thanked him, blessed him, and went out. Her first thought was to relate this to the boys, but as she drove the thought occurred to her that it is a terrible thing to live in the shadow of prophecy, and she resolved to keep it in her heart.

iv

The youthful mind, whatever it may darkly glimpse of eternity's weight, does not often bear it long. It was thus in the main a pleasant time for Roman. He was grateful then for the week's rhythm, for his cast of calculable teachers and assignments. And in the semblance of resumed regularity those things which had been lost became more apparent.

Chiefly he realized a kind of contradiction in the fact that much as he enjoyed Francis's company he hadn't actually spent any time with his friend away from school since the night before the evacuation. Certainly, the hector of the period excused this oversight, but remembering Aunt Sarah's advice and wondering why he should need excuses in the first place, he called Francis one Saturday morning. They arranged a visit for that afternoon, and both hung up the phone relieved.

Francis and his family were living then in his grandmother's home in one of the suburbs across the River from New Orleans known collectively--and not infrequently pejoratively--as the Westbank.

For reasons as plain as time and as difficult of explication, Roman had never been able to cross to the Westbank without a vague melancholy settling from his mind into his stomach in some strange procession of nonbeing. It may simply have been that he'd always feared heights and depths and dark water and that the bridge would thus have made a fine place for forcing him to any confession or perjury. He suspected, however, a still more sinister rationality at work, and he felt a mild civil vindication of his sensibility in the fact that while passage to the Westbank was free, a toll was levied on the leaving. In short, Roman and most of the boys he knew viewed the Westbank with extreme prejudice.

Francis's grandmother lived in one of the older, more respectable neighborhoods of old Algiers, its straight streets lined with oaks and crossed every day by the long strides of the bridge's shadow. Its residents were sociable, hard-working, mainly elderly. Nonetheless, Francis had also since early boyhood conceived a deep disdain for this place which for a year following the storm he would be forced to designate home.

The house itself, a welcoming two-story of ivy-lined brick, could well have fit an English farm. Within, though, its rooms spread in dim, cold, cluttered conveyance, as though the tenants, disabused of their British aspirations by the semi-tropics, had nonetheless contrived to introduce an Anglican clime. To Roman it bore the dismal air of a chipped shell, no longer luminous, slipping about in the wrack, its builders deceased. And within it the lady of the house, like a translucent fish calmly taking shelter, drew slowly nearer the shore. She had always shown Roman an exceeding kindness, yet she seemed distant, as though withdrawn in self to some far-off plain. She seemed hardly to have noticed that one of her sons and his children had moved in with her.

It was in the dry, dim recesses of her retreat, perfumed with antiquity, that Francis had wandered through distant forums of song into a darkened aesthetic, inscrutable to Roman's pedestrian sensibility.

Music, always near the center of Francis's existence, had become his point of connection with the world, an indefinite sea in whose possibility he floated, cocooned against and affirmed concerning matter's stridence. As usual, he was generous in his interests and sought to share the fruit of his exploration with Roman, so that when Michael and Andrew retired to the second floor, Francis and Roman moved to the corner of the den where the computer screen glowed against the dark curtain drawn on the window to the back yard.

There broke over them now a whirr of insectine clicks and chirps as the old computer lurched into the web. Francis's hand flashed up at the first harsh note and in the consequent silence whispered (evidently unnecessarily), "She always does that. Thinks if she can't hear it it's not working."

It was not the last time the boys would sit thus; often in the sun room of Francis's renovated home, palmettos waving in the bright breeze without, Roman, rarely enthusiastic in his dilettante, would feign some portion of his interest in his friend's diligent researches. And it was perhaps this mediation, this chance to sit and together gaze on some other, which prolonged their time together. Yet now, as this first time Francis led Roman an animated tour of his recent discoveries--absurdist music videos, the arcana of lesbian confessions, images muted and set against black backgrounds, scripts inscrutably lurid--Roman shriveled. He felt himself suddenly party to some vast excavation, a violent prying up of floorboards for the sake of gazing angrily on nothing and declaring the triumph of beauty.

Before long Francis, evidently discerning his friend's dimmed enthusiasm, suggested they move upstairs. In his temporary room with its white blinds drawn on the dismal scene without, Francis picked his way among the loose laundry to a stereo atop the cedar dresser. Turning back toward Roman, who lingered near the door, he pressed a button and said, "Let's listen."

Roman assumed the music would serve as background to their conversation and, laughing to himself, prepared to deliver an anecdote he'd recently gleaned from a teacher. It concerned a herd of Grecian goats who in the low hills between Olympia and Patras had earned themselves a reputation for unsolicited overtures. But as the music began Francis, seated on his bed, leaned against the headboard, his eyes shut. Roman took a hard wooden chair against the wall and resting his head on the yellow paper shut his eyes as well.

Only slowly and by tortuous courses of the imagination did his ears approach this fresh cacophony. He found himself swept by the dissonance of bells and the unsettled beating of the bodiless heart into sudden flights of the blood; more than once he started, returning to himself through a flood of surreal suggestions dislocated entirely from his small fund of experience.

Thus passed some thirty minutes. Often Roman felt his friend's eye; now his voice slanted through the malign air. "You don't like it, do you?"

Flushed, hoping to rise, Roman replied, "Not all of it, anyway."

Francis smiled. "No worries. It usually takes about five times before I start to like this sort of thing."

Roman had long taken his musical direction from Francis. Left to himself he should have discerned solely by pleasure. But for Francis there were limits, strict qualitative measures of musical merit. Roman had slowly molded his taste to those limits, forcing himself to eschew what he should else have enjoyed if only for fear of his friend's rebuke. Here though Francis seemed to delve into an inner darkness, a secret space shrouded in white sheets whose edges fluttered still in the storm's wake. Myrmidon though he was, he drew back before the musing.

To his great relief they then crossed the landing to Andrew's room, where their brothers had devised a pulley system of string, tape, and coat hangers so that from bed Andrew might operate the room's three light switches. His eye, passing over the room's several orderly shelves of books, the creaseless blue bedspread, the white microscope on its immaculate desk, was drawn to a large book which lay open on the grey carpet. Stepping closer as Francis proposed a game of football, he found himself drawn into a painting. By a line of small rowboats declining, sinister to center, as well as by the dim dawn-shrouded shapes of masts and spars, he took the blue argent vista for a harbor. He would, perhaps, have found it soothing but for a grigious air of industry evinced by the scene's sun, which though it cast against the upper canvas an empyrean glow nonetheless burned itself as a single red eye. Its gravity consumed.

Before he could look further the three called him to come, and the four boys descended to the quiet street and divided into their usual teams: Roman and Andrew against Francis and Michael. The division was in part one of necessity: that by age brought boredom, that by fraternity a disproportionate tension.

The yard being insufficient, they played in the street, and its traffic, though spare, called for the occasional cessation. Francis, with hyperbolic neighborly feeling, waved at each passing driver. The first two waved cordially if a bit bemusedly back. The third did not, and as the boys moved back into the street, Francis raised a curved finger to the retreating bumper and yelled, "---- you!" Roman, assuming comedy, began accordingly to laugh until, turning toward his friend, he started and nearly stepped back at the anger in his eye.

"What the heck was that for, Francie?" Michael asked. He had always been more direct than Roman and had observed Francis's rage from the first.

"That guy was an -------. He didn't even wave back."

"Who cares? He probably didn't even see you."

"Well, he should have. God damn ------- needs to pay attention."

"You know what, Francis, you're the -------."

"Michael!" Roman shouted. "Come on, let's just play." Secretly he sided with his brother, but his interior division left him no energy for argument, and he sought to turn his attention wholly to the game. The next goal would win; he and Andrew held the ball some twenty yards from the end zone. Briefly they conferred.

"Short?" Andrew asked.

"No, let's just try to wrap it up. Think you can throw it far enough?"

"Should be able to. No guarantees where it's going."

The play began. Roman dallied about the line of scrimmage and then, as Francis neared, burst for the goal line. Francis knew the scheme and stuck close as Andrew heaved the ball in a high, slow arc several yards to Roman's left. Roman cut toward it, and the anger that had flooded the boys' consciousness drove them into continuous collision as they strove for position. At last they leapt together. The ball glanced from Francis's fingers, and Roman, falling now, stretched and cradled the dusty leather to himself as together the boys tumbled to the concrete, Francis landing more or less on top of him. Panting, they rose, and Francis turned away. The smile that had taken root in Roman's eye dissipated, his pupils contracting as he stared at the back of Francis's neck. He thought that his friend's eye, whirling away, had betrayed a renewed anger, a distillation of the curse he had cast on the unaware stranger.

v

To his further discomfiture, Roman found that he was not alone in his detections. He and Michael had departed shortly after the game's conclusion, and as they crossed the toll bridge back to New Orleans, his father asked what was wrong with Francis.

"Nothing, far as I know." A familiar contraction commenced in his gut.

"Don't you think he's gotten kinda...dark? I started feeling depressed just looking at him. And what's with the wrist bands?" His voice had grown louder, his tone distinctly accusative.

Roman explained that they were mere tokens of friendship. He had expected his parents to see in them some black significance and hurried to dismiss their concern.

"Well, they look like crap."

"That's for sure," chimed Michael, laughing, chin resting suddenly on the seat back. And the last word had been said.

vi

Yet the haunting would continue.

The following weekend Ignatius Prep played its first football game since the storm. The stadium was near the Morans' temporary address, and Roman had invited Francis to watch the game and stay for dinner. Francis's parents would bring the boys to the stadium; Roman's parents would bring them home.

Roman's parents were away when Mr. and Mrs. Higgins knocked on the door. Simon Tan, though, the proprietor, happened to be present, along with his son, Michael, a boy just younger than Roman who suffered with certain developmental defects. His head was just disproportionately large, his back slightly hunched. He was his father, thrust back through several steps of evolution. When the knock came he was seated on the floor in his room upstairs; he now paused in perusing his vast collection of baseball cards (his knowledge of statistics was encyclopedic). Dimly he grasped the house, his house, was not now his house, the knock on his door not for him almost never for him anyway. Still, his house, and he loomed down the dark stair into the pale sunlight in the foyer as Roman opened the front door.

Mrs. Higgins, surprised at this unaccounted for personage, asked in an uncertain voice, "Is that you, Michael?" (She hadn't been home when Michael and Roman had visited.)

Roman, attempting to explain and doing so too slowly, said, "This is Michael…"

"Wow, you look…different."

"God, that's not Michael," Mr. Higgins said. "Come on, let's go."

And Michael was left standing in the hall, confused as to their "Michael?". He was, after all, Michael.

vii

Ten minutes later Roman and Francis disembarked at John Thompson Stadium, a concrete fixture ideal for high school athletics, utterly impervious to any serious vandalism, natural or willful. The bands adorned Francis's wrists again; from his lean frame hung a black shirt blazoned in the heraldry of metal bands. In the sight of his friend thus attired Roman had immediately intuited his mother's black glances. As nothing could be done for the moment, though, he turned to the immediate difficulty of finding a seat as they stepped out squinting into the shadeless concrete stands.

The football team in those days could claim little for itself. Forty years had passed since they'd taken any title, ten since they'd appeared in the playoffs. They threw the ball little, largely for interceptions; they ran little better. The boys themselves were, in the main, small, and battered on both sides of the ball. Their kicks rarely cleared the goalposts; their punts often achieved negative results. Partly in defense against embarrassment, partly from common conviviality, the games had become little more than pretext for society, the contest on the turf attended less intently than the flux of faces at the foot of the stands.

Whatever awkwardness the boys may have felt as they stood for a moment scanning the spare crowd, however, resulted more from imagination than from any actual attention they may have drawn. For Roman and Francis still enjoyed a certain anonymity. They had found a small circle of friends and, had they chanced upon them, would have greeted them gladly; otherwise they considered to themselves, quite rightly, that the onus of recognition lay with their less familiar classmates. At any rate, they had soon passed below the bulk of the crowd and climbed to a row of unoccupied seats.

The early afternoon was cool, though between breaths of wind the sun made itself felt. Roman glanced repeatedly at Francis's legs, his knees pink through the torn denim.

"I don't know how you can wear jeans all the time."

"It's comfortable. Feels like a warm bath."

"Baths make me sweat. Always feels like I need a shower."

"Sometimes you say the most helpful things."

"Ah, look, Muller!"

Fr. Muller, typically to be found pacing the sidelines during a game, had taken a turn in the stands and was passing below them. Francis had developed a sort of bombastic rapport with the priest.

"Mullerrrr!" he called.

Father Muller glanced up, spotted the source of the uncouth call, and, shaking his head in amusement, climbed the concrete steps to the boys' perch.

"Afternoon, gentlemen."

"Hello, Father."

"You're looking more dissolute than usual, Mr. Higgins. You notice, by the way, that I didn't just shout 'Higgins' at you like some kind of frat house goon."

"You were so far away down there. And you know, it's not so good being an Ignatius boy. I get home on the weekends and don't know how to dress myself. You clergymen are privileged."

"So I'm told, Mr. Higgins, again and again."

"Sure, sure, offer it up, Father."

"And how are you, Mr. Moran?"

"Alright, thanks. Think we've got a chance?" He raised his chin toward the field.

Muller turned an infidel eye. "Speaking as school president I say we can always succeed. Speaking as dispassionate observer I say 'hell no'."

The boys, squinting up at him, burst into laughter. He took them in for a minute more with his odd, downturned smile. "Well, gentlemen, enjoy the afternoon," he said finally. They watched as his hunched shoulders bounced back down the steps and shuffled off through the crowd again, inclining here and there to the members of his vast acquaintance. Roman imagined that Francis, by some odd contrariety, was the priest's favorite of those present.

Meanwhile the opposing team had scored three touchdowns. Presently one of the Ignatius offensive linemen became a projectile in the hands of a monstrous linebacker. This would be the lineman's last game. No one in the stands, not even the boy's parents, saw what happened.

Three slightly younger boys now approached Roman.

"Big R! What's going on?" the smallest of them asked, his long blonde curls bouncing as he nodded in enthusiastic greeting.

"Hey y'all. This is my friend Francis."

None of them greeted Francis. Francis greeted none of them. Roman experienced a sudden desire for a monk's cell.

"Rome, you see that chick down there?" The second boy, of middling build and Cajun twang, glanced down the stands to a tall, thin girl, pale with raven hair and harsh blue eyes. Roman and Francis had, as a matter of fact, taken independent notice of her.

"Sure, what about her?"

"She wants you," said the third, eyes widening in lewd conspiracy.

"Yeah bro, she wants you like a -----," said the first, laughing.

The blood was in his cheeks now. "Alright, come on, cool it."

"I'm not messing with you, man, that's what her friends said."

"Is she your age?"

"Yeah man, but look at that..."

"Nope, nope, don't wanna hear it. Hit the road, guys."

"But..."

Through their lewd rookery Roman felt a rising redness along with a sudden defensive insanity until he shouted the first word that came to mind.

"HIAWATHA!!!"

And the three, exchanging glances of some concern, took their loud, swaggering way, offensive as boys convinced of their manhood can be.

"What the hell, dude," Francis asked. His gaze, averted through the interlude, had not yet returned.

"They're just some kids from Michael's summer team."

"Geez, so that's what your summer was like."

"It's not so bad in the bleachers."

"Uh-huh... Anyway, she's a good-looking girl."

Roman flushed again. Thirteen or not she was definitely a good-looking girl and even the rumor of her interest raised his opinion of himself. Every day between classes he listened to reports of condoms used, seductions concluded, etc., etc., in catalogs of conquest which he assured himself proceeded largely from the action of excess hormones on defective imaginations; nonetheless the talk aroused in him a kind of competitive spirit which liberally influenced his own excesses and deficiencies. Sex had never come close to him and if it had he wasn't sure what he should have done. At any rate he felt that here he must demur if only for the sake of decorous if not ethical considerations.

"She's ok."

"Sure."

Roman looked at her again and, in a brief flash, saw her as though perfected. It was the feminine counterpart to his picturing men in mustaches. Often, glimpsing a woman's face in, say, a passing car, his eye transfigured the features so that he saw not the woman, not even as she ever had been or would be, but as it were the form of woman contracted to such a body. He was in consequence constantly falling in love, at least until the woman herself appeared in the plain light.

He was shaken from dream by Francis's chuckling.

"What?"

"'Hiawatha?'"

"I don't know."

They resumed their silent vigil.

viii

The loss that day was spectacular. The team's offense had accrued thirty-seven yards. The defense had allowed seven hundred. When at last the whistle rang its silver relief, the scoreboard marked a stark 84-0 against the sky. Perhaps half of those filing out took notice.

Much more depressing, Roman considered, was the fact that nothing now remained between his mother and Francis. She had always seemed to dislike Francis in proportion as she liked the rest of his family. She found his musical taste disgraceful, his person unhygienic. She had once during their commute to elementary school heard him say he'd like to have long hair in college; consequently, Roman was reminded--at staggering length--of his status as representative of his parents and grandparents and everybody back to Adam and that his choice of friends could jeopardize his future, temporal and eternal. She saw Francis as external principle of all discord between herself and her son.

The look on his mother's face, a flat stare fit to leave Pacino jealous, confirmed Roman's apprehensions as the boys approached her car. Roman had never quite discerned whether her apparent lack of control over her expressions arose from complete artlessness or from some sense of her justification. He had developed two means of counteracting her moods, one of insolence, the other of unrelenting cheer. He chose the latter now, both from a sense of propriety and from an instinct toward the moral high ground. He smiled as he entered the car, plied her unceasingly with questions about her day, her friends, the parish, her mother, until they had safely reached home. He knew the presence of Michael and his father would ease the situation but only till the arrival of Francis's parents. His manner grew sullen, therefore, as dinner passed. His heart seized and blood rushed to his face at the sound of a horn outside. Francis of course had recognized the chill mounting around the table and vanished as quickly as he could without seeming to retreat.

The door closed and Roman, having walked his friend out, stared at its white surface for a moment, feigning fascination with a thin crack in the paint. He turned back toward the dinner table, studiedly avoiding his parents' eyes as he resumed his seat. He sat in silence, knowing his parents would shortly ask Michael to leave the room and wanting only for the inevitable discussion to be past.

"Michael, give us a minute, would you?" his father asked.

Michael stood, eyes apprehensive. He was the only one unaware of what waited, and he left the room quickly, disturbed that something evidently had been wrong without his knowing.

Roman's mother rose, aggressive, carbonated and shaken. "How can you go out in public with someone who looks like that?"

They were in the open now and Roman felt the anger rise. "What did you want me to do? Tell his parents to drive home so he could change?"

And she, righteous, eyes narrowed, one hand on hip, the other leveled at his eye: "Don't you *dare* have an attitude with me."

And he again, still confident: "I'm not having an attitude. I'm seriously asking you what to do when *my* friend doesn't look the way *you* want him to."

And she, shifting: "There are people we know who might have seen you there. What if Fr. Muller would've seen you with him wearing those disgusting wrist bands?"

And he, with heavy hand, smiling: "We *did* see Fr. Muller. We talked to him for ten minutes. He loves Francis."

And she, retiring, despairing; the father advancing in her place: "Look, Roman, we just have a responsibility to make sure you spend time with the kind of people who are worth while."

And he, angry again, offended: "What, do you expect me to just go up to him and say, 'Hey, sorry, we can't be friends anymore because my mom thinks you're a bad person'?"

And the mother breaking in: "He looks like an addict!"

And the father, calm, exasperated: "Eloise. Of course not, but maybe it's time to let things run their course. I mean, I asked Francis's dad what he thinks of Ignatius, and he said he thinks they're a little over the top with the 'men for others thing.' That's just not right. And it's not like you, is it?"

"He doesn't have to be like me to be my friend."

"No, but you tend to be like him. And at a certain point we have to make sure that doesn't happen."

"But can't I help him to be better?"

"Do you think that's happening at all?"

"I think so."

A silence followed. Roman felt the blood beating along his jawbone. His father stared at him, thoughtful. His mother shifted from foot to foot, cheeks splotched pink, eyes rolling right, then left, small with tears.

"Ok," his father said.

Roman looked up, sensing change. His mother looked, too, aghast.

"We," his father continued, looking at his mother, "will stay out of it for now. You know how we feel about the situation, but you're right."

"Ok." He felt the anger still but recognized his gains and resolved to keep them.

The conversation would not be resumed explicitly for some years, but it remained, a silent subtext carried on in a look here, an absence there, and above all in a feeling running strong and insistent through Roman's thoughts that he must protect Francis from his parents and above all from himself.

ix

The day before Thanksgiving arrived and with it the last evening of classes. Essential repairs had been completed in Mid-City, and the school would resume its life there after the holidays. Much of the building would remain unusable, and the student body entire would not be reunited at Banks Street until after Christmas; as such, the return inspired a sense of beginning and ending which bound each to each, and the excitement of an expedition enlivened every class that evening.

After six weeks, too, Simon Tan had found he needed to return to his Metairie address. Already, though, an elderly couple, the Merics, known to Eloise in connection with her esoteric errands, had offered the Morans the use of their country house, a five-bedroom mansion on ten acres, one of the latter devoted to a pond stocked with bass and bluegill. They accepted, partly of necessity, for Jack had begun to be ashamed at their dependence. They had grown used to change, though, and familial merriment had grown as the move had drawn nearer.

Thus, while Roman sat through his last evening of classes, the rest of the family had moved their few belongings across the lake. It was the one move of the seventeen they endured and enjoyed that year from which Roman was exempt. When the final bell chimed at ten o'clock that evening, he walked out, buoyant with his confreres' holiday excitement, into the cold and heavy air

His mother picked him up at their customary corner a block from campus; as she waited, her slight unease at crossing the lake so late had swelled at the sight of distant lightning glowering in the west. Nonetheless, her humor was good. Their new quarters, as she had expected, stood already richly dight in icon, cross, and relic; she had that morning removed her surreptitious crucifix from Simon's wall, relieved to wrest self and Savior's image from their heathen housing. Then, too, good will had been restored between herself and Roman. A week had passed since their argument, and he, partly from a feeling of remorse, partly from fear of an unbearable hour in the car, had the day before written her a letter of apology and appeal. His own excitable nature set against his mother's had always rendered conversation between them difficult. They communicated better at a distance, and he felt his latest effort had been his best. She felt so as well, as evidenced by the oyster po-boy awaiting him in the back seat. Appetite sharpened by excitement, he fell to and finished by the time they had reached the dark lake.

The Causeway, which connects New Orleans to its more conservative suburbs on the north shore of Lake Pontchartrain, was at that time the longest super-aqueous bridge in the world. Roman would in the coming nine months become so expert in the bridge's nuances that he could look up, even years later, and say precisely which mile he was crossing without recourse to the markers.

On this night, though, he paid the miles no attention. The storm rising steadily in the West fascinated him. Its blackness, burnt with sudden lightning, swelling from itself and swallowing the stars, struck him with a strange comfort. It seemed to bear the hope of a new world flashing out of nothing. His mother felt no such comfort. She gripped the wheel tighter and tighter as the wind whipped the tires, her thin knuckles whitening until they seemed to glow in the dim dash lights. No stars were visible by the time they reached the bridge's midpoint, but a faint green light rose here and there above the water.

Roman, like most youth knowing he would die without believing it, wondered what fish lay nestled at the bases of the pilings. He had always wondered about them, how many sheltered there in the dark, their sizes and species and whether they wondered at all at the endless change above them. He grew worried only once, when the car rose over the draw bridge eighteen miles in. He imagined each time they gained the peak and the wheels buzzed across the iron grate that there replaced the concrete, more or less vividly in keeping with conditions, that it would give out and depth and dark water consume him. It was one of the places--and these, though he knew nothing of it, were many--where his and his mother's imaginations met in darkness.

At length they left the bridge, and the wind calmed in the arms of the pine woods stretching for hundreds of miles on each side. They passed in silence through the small cities above the lake, the lights of their just-burgeoning economies dim with the night's age and blurred slightly by the still-driving rain. A high and narrow bridge bore them over a thin black band of river, and at last they entered the country by a curving road bound in by longleaf pines. The streetlights grew less and less frequent until at last they vanished altogether. The headlights glared against the heavy rain and Eloise slowed more and more with the unfamiliar way. More comfortable cars raced by her or pulled up close behind, their high beams blinding in her mirrors. After a quarter of an hour they turned onto what felt like a dirt lane strewn with loose gravel. The moon's face shone shaded through the thinning clouds racing East, and in its inconstant light Roman dimly discerned the outline of a large house broken by what seemed a huge oak tree. They soon pulled up below its branches before a yellow-lit porch which stretched the length of the house.

Roman's father waited on the porch swing. With a relieved air he rose and, hands in his pockets, shuffled to the head of the steps.

"I've been trying to call y'all. Radio said they closed the bridge."

Less wearied, Eloise might have engaged in retroactive hysterics. Instead she simply said, "Guess we just made it on."

"How bad did it get?"

"I think I said about five rosaries."

"I think I saw a waterspout," Roman broke in.

"When?" his mother sighed.

"It was close to the end. I didn't think you'd wanna know."

They crossed the threshold. Roman gathered a brief but pleasant impression of the living room--deep couches lit by several lamps in amber shades, walls of books and their worn fragrance, billiard and ping pong tables, and an iron spiral staircase--before Michael caught him up in a burst of chatter about the house and the weather and the animals he'd seen outside during the day. He hurried Roman up to his bedroom, a comfortable nook on the home's east end. A lamp glowed at each side of the bed, and in the quiet light Roman felt himself very weary and suddenly somewhat sick. He had grown in the preceding months accustomed to sleeping in unusual rooms; nonetheless he found himself now, for the first time, missing his own bed. Normally he should not have slept in this one without a thorough preliminary inspection of the premises against insects, particularly spiders, odd smells, and questionable stains. Tonight, though, he called goodnight to his family, took off his uniform, and lay in the instant dark which slowly brightened under the influence of stars burning through the lone window radiating cold across the room.

V.

ALIVE ALONG WITH YOU

And then down to the sea, over the vivid city's raining bay, and the Sunday's final hour arrived. Down in the brown water a little apart from his cousins he sat beside the piled stones watching absently the waves echoing the slow sure swell along the sand and through his red, green trunks. And he pried the small clams clinging to the jetty, the high stones white in the sun slowly darkening descending through immotion to the bay where down in the brown water his mind moved at the tips of his fingers.

Slowly the fingers softened in the warm salt, and the fine-edged clams rasped at the pruning tips touching, testing, working the loose like teeth and piling the dislodged caked in silt in the red cup treasured above the slow waves only to take life from the basement of memory even below the pilings.

And the blonde there thus (the purpose otherwise affirmed) lay staring through the spread arms of the oaks and closer the black lenses on sky reflected unmoving in the bikini's ecstasy and the children knew no danger. And he saw her not only as she was above the water but also in the tributary gazes passing on the sand-blown brick above the beach. Then to share himself and prove a boy's power past the measure of men he stood dripping in the shade at her side tilting the red rim to her eye as she tilted back the glass in pale green discovery to say they were beautiful.

And the clams came home without their knowing and sat in the sun at the window in the red light of the cup as he slept in the car curving quickly through the pines around the Gulf so that when at last relieved yet sad with that always last day they parked below the blooming red maple the stench had started and sharpened to the point of punishment past the mere repudiation though his fingers still were tender and in places torn with plucking them from the rocks below the waves.

i

Roman woke, for reasons past his understanding, before light, and, unable after half an hour or so to resume his sleep, found a restroom at the top of the stairs and relieved himself. Chill air flowed freely through the worn seal of the frosted window, and he shivered as at his uncertain touch frigid water burst from the shower head. Despite his doubts the water soon warmed, and as the first cloud of steam unfurled he piled his clothes on the white tile floor. For three minutes he stood in the hot rain, dazed, head aching as with addiction, stomach uneasy. At a slight movement to his right he turned and, heart lurching painfully into waking, flinched at the sight of a large black spider perched just beside him on the yellow curtain. Remaining distant as he could he cupped his hands, held them to the faucet, and doused his sudden foe. The spider whirled to the floor of the tub and slid inexorably toward the drain where, thanks to its size, it caught for a moment, writhing madly until the shower's stream, now full upon it, forced it into the plumbing. Roman stood trembling, breathing with difficulty in the humid air as he stared for a spindle's hint of revenance; nauseated in his fixation, he shut off the water, stepped onto the shaggy dun bathmat, and raised the window an inch. The cool air, mingling with the sight of a strip of fallow field across which coursed a large, shaggy black dog, began to calm him.

The fine dust of the landing floor clung to his soles as he crossed back to his bedroom, where he wiped his feet, twice each, on the short carpet before dressing. Recrossing the landing, he woke Michael, who had until that year been always an early riser and who still, when touched, sat up immediately, blinking and staring wide-eyed around him in an attitude of rather comic alert.

As with their parents the two boys maintained a quiet economy between each other; silently they agreed in privileging Thanksgiving above most other holidays. Behind lay the bulk of the fall, while ahead loomed but three weeks of work lightened by the trees' swelling burden of bulbs. The weather, generally, had begun to be dependably cool, while the chill mists and fevers of February remained at some remove. And then the feasts, cornucopiate buffets whose component dishes and delicacies had so accumulated in the Moran and Schiro traditions that only the most liberal hermeneutics on moderation even in moderation could pardon the revelers their multiple counts of gluttony.

Today, in its straitened time, there beckoned but one feast. Before that would be Mass, and before the preparations thereto remained a free hour with which the boys stole downstairs in the hope of exploring their new property, as they considered it.

They moved in the taut, chuckling silence of youthful conspiracy. Each iron creak on the spiral stair, the squeak of the cherrywood floor, the rasp of the lock sharpened in them the fear that their mother would wake and detain them. Once over the threshold they considered themselves safe and broke into a mischievous run, thundering briefly along the blue wooden porch (at which point their mother did indeed wake up), and leaping the three steps to the red dirt circular drive where the cars huddled below the expansive oak Roman had dimly perceived the prior night.

The sun was just up, and though the night had been chill and the ground lay hard and wet from storms, the breathless sky promised a warm Thanksgiving, always a melancholy possibility in New Orleans.

The parcel of land the boys now surveyed stretched over ten acres from the road to the woods, most of it pasture with one or two small farm buildings, grey with age and battered. These they eschewed, rightly assuming them cluttered, dark, and redolent of rats. On the eastern edge of the land, where the still-cool sun peered shyly through a dense band of pine and oak and cedar, nestled in the crook of the woods, sat the small pond, silver and smoking in the dawn. They ran to it, slowed, and, bending, studied its banks, riddled with deer tracks and egrets' glyphs. They jumped lightly onto the old grey dock and peered into the still water, opaque with the sun's obliquity, spitting onto the surface to see if any bluegill should rise and smack at their frothing offerings.

No fish were forthcoming, and the boys next turned to the woods. Cautiously they padded down a thin levee between the trees and the water, peering through the trunks into the increasingly bright spaces between. A faint breeze began to rise, and as its breath wafted through the forest, they caught a chill, fresh scent of peppermint which would in many distant woods call Roman back to those.

They came upon a favorable entry, a slight thinning of the undergrowth as if where a path once had lain. (It was, in fact, an old deer path, resolving into wood as the deer retreated further into the trees.) They pushed through the clumps of sapling oaks and cedars, showers of dew and last night's rain dampening their jeans, then scrambled over the trunk of a fallen pine and doubled back beneath the trunk, pushing through the thin, dense band but always, it seemed, below that fallen pine held up in a dozen places by its standing companions. Roman felt the weight of their burden; he hurried on, afraid of being pressed into service.

Passing through a thick screen of firs, the boys stood suddenly blinking in the sun. A new landscape, unexpected and inviting, stretched ahead of them. The trees, here mainly cedars, thinned, and a yellow grass grew lush and buoyant underfoot. All was dry in the unbridled breeze and light. The mint scent, sharpened as if by water's touch, blew freely from the next band of woods a mile to the east. They had moved now into neighboring land, though they saw no house or sign of use. They would visit this place daily in the coming months and it would come to seem to them another country, enchanted but barren, in which they moved as kings and exiles.

The birds, silent while the boys had toiled through the woods, now resumed their argent measures. The tones of woodpeckers, least familiar, were most apparent, and the occasional jungle laughter of the Pileated heightened the grove's exotic air. Olive and lazuli clashed in thought at the mingled phrases of Phoebes and Jays, and the roseate tones of the doves' down glowed in their dawning deliberations.

A slight ridge, perhaps six feet higher than the surrounding ground, enclosed the grove to the south, and the boys, stilled till now by the sudden revelation, turned to it, mounted for vantage, and followed it down the grove's edge. Blue seeds brightened the cedar bushes, and the ground lay soft with red maple leaves fallen in the night's wind. Black squirrels, much larger than any of the grey relatives known to the boys, rushed about in the short pines and scrub oaks on the ridge, their heavy bodies bowing the thin limbs when they leapt, their white faces flashing as they chattered.

They came then to the end of the ridge, which sloped back down to the floor of the grove, here opening into a wide plain, clear-cut and yellow with long grass undulant in the breeze. Down the plain marched massive power lines in infinite gesture, dull gray, unmuted by the ascendant sun. Between the boys and this meadow intervened a grey-green gash in the earth, a sort of ravine only about twelve feet deep and perhaps thirty wide but with exceedingly steep sides, evidently the bed of a once assertive river where now a clear creek ran, rarely deeper than eighteen inches, populous with small fish and suggestive to Roman of deeper pools, shaded by long limbs reflected by gar. They stood and looked a while into the water where the minnows swam, translucent, less substantial than their own newly created shadows sliding along beneath them, and at the white sand interspersed with the litter of late autumn and the questing roots of the oaks. The boys looked at each other and then turned back, knowing their mother, jittery with her second cup of coffee, would by now have begun to grow anxious for their return.

ii

That year, for the first time Roman could remember, his mother had insisted in an almost brutal act of faith that her family attend Thanksgiving Mass. Her mind ran always clear on such counts; she had been a math teacher in her first career and the calculus of grace functioned in terms plainly discernible to her, whatever she might feel.

At any rate they piled into the old Suburban and drove back toward town, turning a few miles before they reached the highway onto the grounds of a Benedictine abbey. They crossed a bridge above a shallow stream, the same, Roman thought, as ran in the ravine, though here swifter and deeper but with the same pellucidity whenever it shot into the sun from under the pines rising at its sides and leaning in toward the vanishing point above its bed.

As they wound along the stone avenue toward the church, Roman's mother turned and said, "Roman, last time you were here you weren't even one." He had expected the retelling; mildly annoyed, he nonetheless smiled.

"Why did we take an infant to midnight Mass an hour from home?" his father asked.

"It was so special!" Her brow furrowed as she flung aside her reply. "But I was trying the whole time not to laugh because this lector had to read the word 'ewes' but she said it 'ee-wees.' And you know when you get the giggles and you just can't stop? That was me the whole time."

They parked among the few other cars in the gravel lot and walked up the white pebble drive toward the church, which rose beside a still lake ringed in crepe myrtles, its brown bricks swelling to white steeples in the clear light above the pines. The facade, gilt in gleaming mosaic, was dominated by the four evangelical emblems, who in their line appeared about to process into the air. The impression was heightened by the fact of a stone foot, hoof, talon, and paw protruding somewhat crudely from each image. The sight, mediated by memories of the classroom, reminded him, as most new things had done in recent days, of Francis and must thereby have darkened his expression in some unintended way, for his mother, always quick to notice such things and take them as affronts against herself or God, whispered sharply, "Just be thankful!" as they passed through the ten foot wooden doors.

That last time Roman had entered this church, of course, lay beyond the scope of his memory, but he had assembled an image of the place to accompany his mother's regular tale, and now the fabricated memory stood corrected inasmuch as it could ever be. Far off stood the high altar under a vast dome, punctuated at its base by clear windows. Above the skylights loomed the apostles and the archangels arrayed around the holy throne from which gazed out with stern eyes and upraised hand Christ as emperor. Nearer stood an altar of white marble. To its right and left, facing each other from their deep cloistral chairs of carved dark wood, the brown-robed monks had gathered. Some knelt. Others craned about or bent to share a word. Most wore thick beards, many glasses. Above and just before them great wooden rafters spanned the aisle into which poured clear, cold light through the tinted blue glass above the murals of the martyrs holding the implements of their ends. Here and there in gold ran Latin inscriptions, and gazing down over the congregation seated in thin pews of pale wood stood saints in white marble and fresco, still vivid, from the hand of an early postulant.

Softly these beauties pressed themselves to Roman's eyes as he began to pray, badly as was his fashion and with a curious connectivity of image. *Thankful sure for what was it? guns new shotguns cheap in cheap cases hard rubber raising hands camouflage locks popping on white carpet bedroom practicing followthrough on wall not dead but blue eyes? green eyes? Our Father what color with flame black at campfire hot dogs urine on embers in turns and smoke through stars or other way is color there and char scent and fork in meat fork in pork fork in York spork spork spork but no the Lord is with why not same now same all day ten years five days four quarters ten years and et in saecula saeculorum still though fourteen but yes fourteen still.*

His prayers ceased briefly at the sudden presence in the next pew of a family with two pretty daughters, more or less his age. Before they could take their seats he had noticed the long curves of their legs below the green hems of their dresses, and an urge to smooth the gooseflesh raced along the tips of his fingers. Their brown curls caught the light, grew gold, transparent, shook sweet scents to him still kneeling. He felt the blood move and by a mild effort aided by the stained light turned his prayers through indirections to Molly.

Chill humors, invitations passed down desks beside the lake to fear of joy of games and instead relief in regret yet now written and writing, the cool blood at the mailbox mother's indiscretions at the door and distance in space in settlement in sign for Kant for Mill the tilting imperative against the hidden Jew yet most useful? what more than no more than what use after all?

A single chime shook him from his desert thoughts as he rose with the rest of the small congregation amid the thick clouds of incense which swelled steadily and curled among the rafters in the light of the upper windows. Roman's eye followed the progress of the crowds to the golden Latin inscriptions. *Quis ut deus...tibi dabo claves...tremendum et fascinans.* He puzzled over their meaning, from a mixture of interest and pride and architecture's intimate directives, nearly until Communion, only dimly aware of the monks' chant and less so of the abbot's homily. He shuffled forward with the rest, his eyes darting into dalliance with each face they met. He received the thick Host hungrily, and afterwards, kneeling on the hard yellow wood, he began at last to be silent. The desperation of his prayer had subsided in the weeks since Francis's agnosticism had begun; nonetheless, sense withdrawn behind his eyes, it was his friend who occupied his mind in its attempts to rise, fluttering its wings weakly like a monstrous moth on the surface of a clear stream, to the eternal other.

iii

Mitchell Schiro, Roman's uncle, lived in testament to activity. He owned a prosperous insurance firm, and he prided himself on being at the office no later than 5:30 each morning. He left no earlier than 6:45 each evening. Rather than a lunch he took a swim from 12:05 to 12:35 each afternoon. Few could judge from the sight of him in a suit that he had very nearly made a career as a football player, but those who saw him in the pool--and not a few envious and admiring eyes had followed his progress in the gym through the years--knew the secret of his endurance. Returning to his desk from the pool he ate a handful of almonds. His secretary had never known him to use the restroom. It was an unusually, almost supernaturally, productive office.

Mitchell's life, however, was not devoid of contemplation. While he swam or made the short drive to and from the office or, as now, waited for his Thanksgiving guests to arrive, he wondered at what he had achieved. He had never held a mortgage. His wife was still beautiful and gave every sign of remaining so. His children followed him in everything, to his taste for Paul Simon and a penchant for plaid turtleneck sweaters.

And yet observers catching him in his quiet moments had discerned a certain discomfiture, a clouding of the massive brow which was perhaps in part the cause of the rumor (most unjust) that white bread and mayonnaise were strictly barred admittance to his house.

For the picture of his achievement was marred by the simple fact that he had not created it entire. His father had become rich from nothing and in turn had barred his sons and daughters from doing the same. Out of an ancient Sicilian obscurity, a line of good and diligent vintners, perhaps, or cobblers, had arisen the great light of Norman Schiro.

On the evening of December 15, 1932, Norman Schiro knelt once again before the toilet and, leaning over its bowl in the yellow light of a bulb swaying gently overhead as on a ship, vomited spaghetti into the dull water.

As he washed his face and blew a bit of gravy from his burning nose, his parents, long used to such outbursts, sat still eating in the chill kitchen. His mother, violent red hair knotted roughly at the back, bathrobe loose, luxurious, pointed a fork wound in pasta at the bathroom door.

"What the hell's his problem, Ange? You ever heard of a Dago don't eat gravy?"

"Hah...my mother'd been grateful for us throwing up. We never had nothin to throw up on." His eyes idled over the paper as his hands robotically ripped thick chunks from a loaf of French bread, wiped up red gravy, and with unexpected delicacy delivered the morsels to his mouth.

"Listen buddy I'm just as poor as you are."

"Hell if I didn't know."

"I shoulda been rich."

"Ya told me so."

The sound of hearty evacuations, momentarily muffled, arose once more.

By the time Norman emerged from his ablutions, the kitchen was empty. His parents' bedroom door was shut. With a deep breath he sat on the couch, relaxed yet elegant, opened a book, and began, "...*castra collocata in faucibus Etruriae*..."

Pictures from his wedding day, precisely fifteen years later, show him smiling broadly between his parents. Neither smiles. Both wear the astonished look of people in clothes more expensive than their cars. Their son has succeeded, to their eternal black and white disappointment.

In the summer of 1732 Henri Goupil, Knight of St. Louis, formerly of New Orleans, formerly of Acadia, formerly of Paris, found himself prisoner to Tomas Oconor, then governor of the Spanish Colony of Texas. While the circumstances of his imprisonment remain to the present foggy, there can be little doubt that the principal share in the concern fell to Oconor's half-caste daughter Laura, who now in the divided shadow of a palm amid the moonlight knelt at the high window of

Henri's cell. For a week they had met in this manner, conveying their thoughts by a hybrid tongue made fluent by the desire born when first their shackled gazes joined their histories and aspirations.

History for him began in the favor of the king, that strange, unmerited agent of deliverance from obscurity. It coursed along the waterways of the still New World in company with Jogues, Juichereau, Iberville, the Iroquois, and included gifts of gold and frankincense in the form of vast tracts of land, later to bear such disparate names as Delacroix and Mobile, and title. Myrrh had not yet come, though it loomed there above him in the dark face lined in moon.

For her in turn Jovian favor had fallen in the form of beauty. The news of her birth, down in the darkness of the tenancy, had spread from hand to hand through the estate until Oconor himself appeared in the hut by dark. And in the candle's light poured upon her face and his he felt for once the pang of love, and the child was taken into her father's home, and of course in time the suitors came, though only this one, not a suitor but a sacrifice bound and dragged, could awaken in her the chilled ember of love.

And now in the darkness she whispered her fierce new pain, and from the moon-chastened darkness of her breast there appeared a length of rope, and for a moment Goupil, thinking she had secured his means of escape from the vale, allowed his despair to take a measure of hope. But then she showed how simply the bars were moved (for Oconor's romanticism had with age grown boundless), and tying the rope to the palm she watched him rise, love swelling to meet him.

Roman, crossing his Uncle Mitch's half-acre lawn thick with sycamores and pines and rising by the four stairs to the green porch where against the white shutter he once had spied a bright green tree frog, knew nothing of family legend. All that lay beyond the reach of his memory lived in the gauze of indistinction wrought by his aunts' and uncles' assertions. And before him for the moment Uncle Mitch was all, waiting at the top of the stairs, his iron-grey hair, embroiled now in its third decade of retreat across his huge head, glinting in the cool light.

"Romaaaaaan, how ya doin, brotha!?" came the customary greeting with which he took Roman's hand. Roman had always found the hand shake surprisingly mild, and he was forever puzzled by Mitch's apparent unwillingness to prolong eye contact. He would in later years begin to suspect this as evidence of a shyness by now almost inconceivable on Mitch's part, beaten down and cowed over five decades of brash seniority and still just gleaming through.

His tone mellowed, the vine's sardonic touch perhaps appearing as he turned now to Roman's father. "How we doin, Jack? Construction good? Whatcha got, couple a birds? Let me show ya something." They walked away together, Jack cradling a turkey breast, wrapped in foil gilded with smoke, in each hand.

A riot of smells had rushed on Roman at his entry, and as he passed through the foyer beneath the stairs into the growing light of the living room the scents intensified and yielded to the eye's discretion. Turkeys, two, twenty-eight pounds each, gleamed gold in the oven's brass bay. Through a sudden wall of steam arose the bubbling surface of a mushroom soup, while beside it contended stuffed mirlitons and seafood pasta and white rice and brown rice and a dark gravy. Crockpots neared overflowing with oyster and cornbread dressing. A twenty-pound pan of lasagna glowed in creamy coruscance in a second oven. On the counter stood gumbo, jambalaya, crab dip, cheeses. There was no art to the meal and while in later years Roman would come to see something tawdry in his family's taste, a lack of any aesthetic principle, he would also never suffer from particularity.

Despite the tongue's various temptations it was the ears which in their whirling passivity produced the wild firmament of his life among the Schiros. It had, in the slow development of personality, now reached a supreme objectivity, a cacophonous perfection which permitted no deviation in the matter of its principalities, so that when, for instance, Roman's Uncle Daniel had passed away and with him the deep Cajun tones torn with emphysema, his cousin Zeke had taken up smoking.

In a family of such emphatic, not to say frightful, voices, Roman had nonetheless always been allowed, without reproach, to exercise his natural reticence. It was a happy concession and one without which he may not have remained overly fond of the Schiros, for his loves, excepting those of certain shared haunts, had begun to diverge from theirs. Already he could not rouse himself as he once had to any show of fervor for the increasingly calculated spectacle of the football game adding its massive plasmic din to the living room. Yet he wondered that despite this garish (the word which continually that noon rose to his mind) element of their taste, each of his family members lived in beauty--Uncle Mitch in the woods, Uncle Mark at the sea, Aunt Maria amid an artful luxury--and that this beauty, however happened upon, had bound itself to each of them and bound him to them as well.

Meandering some moments among the twittering crowds Roman met Aunt Maria, his godmother. She was a large woman who carried her excess well and seemed thoroughly to enjoy her standing as the only one of her siblings not to have had children. Nonetheless an aura of maternal energy had drawn to her a great company of godchildren, and she missed no opportunity to lavish her abundance on them, returning from her voyages, numerous as they were diverse, laden with meticulously picked and packaged presents. There was thus a mercenary element to Roman's love for her which, in a young boy, need not diminish its ardor. He hugged her, silver jewelry pressing into his chest and cheek and back as her warm, purple scent broke upon him along with the nasal majesty of her voice, which, eschewing the standards of the populace, took precisely as long as it wanted over each syllable.

"Heyyyyy Roman, how ya doin, baaaaby?"

"Great, thanks--happy Thanksgiving."

"Happy Thanksgivin' to you, too." With a half-expected movement she reached into her crocodile handbag and withdrew a small white box.

Opening it, he recognized the tooth of a Great White Shark. What Maria wanted was always hers, yet whether from a sense of duty or an intuitive charity she had ever let others' loves form the fabric of her love for them. Roman had since earliest awareness nursed a fascination with sharks. Once on his birthday, as the two pored over a fossil shop's wares, Roman, emboldened by a nascent sense of her largesse, had asked if she would buy him a certain tooth priced at six hundred dollars. Laughing, she had refused, yet the two had made a pact that day that instead they would, when he was old enough, visit Australia and dive with Great Whites off the Great Barrier Reef. She smiled now, seeing his pleasure in the tooth.

"So you don't forget our deeal."

"Thanks, Aunt Maria, I won't."

Neither forgot, though her death a decade later delayed the execution.

At that moment Uncle Mitch called her away with a question about the soup she'd left bubbling on the stove, and Roman, alone again, felt his loneliness, and meandering once more through the now menacing crowd, exited by the back door. Skulking down the brick steps, he quickened his pace across the back yard to the clear green pond where he had learned almost ten years before to fish for largemouth bass. He stood in a warm patch of sun beneath the pond's circling pines and watched as bass and bluegill swam just outside the lush band of hydrilla along the water's edge. In the center of the pond, where sheets of sun fell in mellow luminance, a bass and bluegill hovered in strange companionship, the translucent flexing of the pectoral fins alone assuring they yet lived.

Behind him rose the slithering crunch of rubber soles on pine needles, and he turned to see, as expected, his father, lips pursed in idiosyncratic smile. It was a smile which in Roman's less generous moods had grown to annoy him, and he turned away.

His father, beside him now, surveyed the still surface and then, turning a half-suspicious glance on him, began, "Everything ok?"

"Yep." He paused for a moment, watching as the gossamer tip of a bass's tail touched the air, delicately waved from side to side, and then dipped without a ripple back below the green-brown glass. "I guess it's just a lot."

His father nodded slightly, eyes fixed as if on something deep beneath the water. "Believe me, I hear ya, they always drive me crazy," he said, evidently thinking of the ravenous family inside, his face by a slight creasing about the eyes betraying a fresh meditation on the grotesque.

"Mm." A tension in his stomach, deepened by awareness of itself, urged him to walk away. The first decade of Roman's life with his father had known an almost desperate closeness, borne perhaps of his knowledge that his father's own father had died young. But his father had lived beyond the years guaranteed, and the fact had made him less and less knowable until Roman, no longer free to speak, found that it was only by some misdirection, usually by way of the outdoors, that he could share his feeling.

"I wish we could fish today." He spoke in a sudden rush of avarice verging on sickness as a bass two feet long slipped by an insolent six feet from shore, seemingly motionless in its animal economy.

"So do I." His father hesitated a moment. "Don't tell Mom I'm telling you this now--it's supposed to be a surprise--but I booked us a duck hunt down around Lake Charles. We're driving down there tomorrow night and hunting Saturday morning."

Roman turned and looked at him, slightly unbelieving. Again his mind balked at this desperado magnanimity. "Seriously?"

"Well, we gotta use those guns sometime." (He had three weeks prior come home, to general astonishment of more and less positive varieties, with three pump-action Remingtons.)

"Thanks, Dad." Excited, he nonetheless continued to gaze on the pond. A maple leaf slalomed to its surface, and as it rested on the clear water a spider skittered from its edge. Suddenly a great bluegill, thick and nearly a foot long, leapt from the water and, diving, swallowed the arachnid as it descended into darkness.

"Woah!" they cried together. Then, knowing they ought to return, the two walked back across the lawn to the large white house where tables, mainly according to age with here and there an amusing exception, had begun to convene.

Roman found himself, without precedent, at a table with several of his aunts and uncles and his grandmother. His appetite, which had sharpened as he entered the house again, now declined once more at the unaccustomed company. The conversation began, as usual, Roman would in the coming years discover, with dramatic commentary on the food.

"Gawwwwd, Maria, this soup is soooo good."

"Yeah, how's a single broad learn to cook like that?"

"Be-*cause*--I have to cook for different men--Benny can't take me out every night."

"Anne, have this gravy at my funeral."

"Jack, a lot of food has gone in this mouth, but this is some of the best ---- I've ever had," Mitch concluded, brandishing a fork laden with turkey breast before dipping it into his rice and gravy. "What'd you think of those blueprints?"

"Looks pretty nice."

"Let me tell you something, you think this house is wide? Wait'll ya see this--three times the size!" He was almost shouting now, his knife and fork describing wide, harsh arcs to capture the glory of his vision.

Aunt Anne and Aunt Maria leaned away from Mitch's implements. Roman glanced about, marveling at the mass of the projected dwelling. His father smirked. "What's he talking about?" Uncle Mark asked his wife. A drama as of the last supper surrounded the Schiro Thanksgivings.

"Daddy would be so proud, Mitch."

"Well, thank you, ya know I just wanna make the old man proud."

"He was always wearing his scapular," interjected Roman's grandmother, the hard line of her outthrust jaw trembling with her comment's incongruous gravity.

"Damn good thing, the way he knocked us around," cackled Uncle Mark. He was a short man, heavy-set and slightly hunched with limping in the wake of a boating accident several years prior. His skin maintained a Mediterranean, even Middle Eastern glow, and his voice, which always began in gravelly, high-pitched tones, rose higher and higher as he told his stories. He resembled an excitable Stalin.

"Y'all remember that time Mitch broke the window and I got the blame? Daddy chased me upstairs and I hid behind the bed. He threw it to one side, I moved over; he threw it to the other side, I moved there. Finally he just picked up the whole damn thing and I can still feel his hand on my ass!"

Mitch laughed with him as the women glanced at each other, severe and Sabine. The conversation halted for a minute, as if confused, then Mitch broached the subject of FEMA and the thread was taken up all around. Roman sat silent, stupefied with food and this brief glimpse of family history, the episodic particulars at such variance with the general encomia. It was a history which grew more obscure to him with each new relation, and it left him increasingly aware of the quality of his blood, of the strains which ran recognizably in him and of those which might lie in wait. He found himself ever more on guard, wary of the self that might some day turn to him and grin.

The sun had ducked behind the woods by the time the uncomfortably full Morans returned to their temporary home that evening. The moon had risen and lay placid and partly hollow in the sky as well as in the still surface of the pond. An owl hooted in the woods, now dry after the day's bright breeze, and a bull frog sat somberly bellowing one of the season's last concerts at the water's edge. Roman's heart rose at each of these revelations but found itself burdened at each turn by the thought that they were not revelations to all, and he could hardly help feeling as he fell into a heavy sleep that something was missing.

iv

For Spencer Zazulak, child of fortune that he was, nothing could be missing. All ever balanced, and in the peaceful cosmic equilibrium there were no holidays save those he could create. Art was the holy, and each day demanded the performance of its lonely and exhilarating offices. He was alive to this responsibility of the initiate as, late that Thanksgiving evening, he entered his Aunt Sylvia's home on Perrier St. He had made plans and would give thanks in the pains of beauty's birth.

His aunt's house stood Uptown, untouched by flood. Well into the second century of its life, it nonetheless lacked none of the improvements of new wealth. There lingered about its well-lit surfaces no sense of decadence--cracked or slanting floors, unsealed windows, sinks creaking, coughing cloudy water--all gleamed and functioned flawlessly in smooth lines and planes and the occasional curve to suggest the infinite, including those of a still life by Caravaggio--an original, of course--which had held Spencer in thrall through many euphoric hours. It was only by the sternest effort of will that he had not applied his improvements to the master's design.

He waited patiently through dinner, politely answering a question when necessary, smiling at a younger cousin to humor her, until the smooth amalgam of wine and conversation had bound the adults in tryptophanic indolence; he then sauntered to the bathroom in the hall, pausing before he opened the door to admire a bust of Aristophanes.

Beyond the door lay a job for a subtle hand. He would not, of course, ply his trade in plain sight. He decided, rather, on a Baroque experiment, a work placed where only he and God (he made here an imaginative concession to his forebears) would know it and measure its delight. Producing a pen from his pocket, he wrote on the baseboard behind the toilet:

Light from light and shite from man,
light in sight of the porcelain can,
hidden from view and bidden to stew
while a true world springs from the ash of the new.

A knock came as he concluded this sublime stanza, so he flushed and washed his hands, feeling he had made the day holy, and took his seat once more at Aunt Sylvia's feast.

v

The stars appeared somewhere beyond Baton Rouge, near the place where I-10 rises once again to plod through the Atchafalaya Basin. Roman sat curled in the back seat of his father's truck, gazing at the luminaries through the large back window. He rarely saw the stars at home, but he had become much more aware of their presence since the storm. He would in deserts to come see them as science had named them, but for now his acquaintance was new and immediate, and his eyes traced constellations of their own design.

From their sidereal transports his thoughts swirled through vague hopes for next morning's hunt and meditations, thrilling in their gentleness, on Molly. Through these musings, like the pang of a familiar illness, flickered Francis, but he had found, with a touch of guilt, that his friend came less to mind as the distance between them increased, whereas wherever he was, at the prompting of a certain slant of light or shade of sky, she came more easily to the surface of thought.

Though he had not heard her voice or seen her face in the past two months, he had written her perhaps once a week. Steadily, and with an exhilarating lack of deliberation, he had disclosed his mind. She, he felt, had done the same, though in her case the mind was so rife with matter beyond itself that she remained essentially distant. Yet the distance manifested in a comforting solidity. There was a system of ideas, a sort of mythology which framed all her thought. And the frame's firmament was God, looming as he had behind Abraham and Isaac on the mountain, indistinct and terrible and exciting;

163

but there was also a more immediate tissue of stories, poems, philosophies, even places which gave avenues of entry to the foundation. She had spent summers in Rome, Christmas breaks in Paris, Easter at Oxford, and everything she saw wove itself into the fabric of her faith like a seamless garment resplendent in its witness.

She rarely wrote of God directly, yet everything she wrote seemed touched with his presence. In Roman's experience most people spoke of things and meant nothing more. One exception was his mother, who for most of his life had seemed incapable of speaking of anything without speaking of God. Here was something entirely new to him, someone who rarely spoke about God but meant him in everything she said, who revealed God to him in everything she touched, the consummation of Midas's wish.

He also took a certain comfort, more exciting and more personal, in the interest she had taken in him, an interest which seemed still to grow. Her salutations had become "Dearest Roman," her valedictions "Affectionately."

In his last letter to her he had explained his recent conflict of belief with Francis, hoping she might offer some insight. He felt more and more that a black gap was widening between him and his friend and that it was his fault, that he had failed to give good example or good counsel or whatever it was Francis needed, failed so spectacularly that he had cost his friend infinite gain. He felt, ultimately, that if God is love and Francis did not believe in God, it could only be for a lack of love, a love that he, Roman, had had a lifetime to offer.

His thoughts were ruptured by a sudden stench followed by a rush of cool air as his father rolled down the window.

"Come on, Dad!" Michael yelled.

"Thought I could get the window down fast enough."

"Well, preempt yourself next time, fat boy," Roman offered.

"Hey, I'm starting my diet tomorrow. And you're looking pretty chunky yourself, boy."

"I need some cushion for that shotgun."

"You need something cause you sure can't hit anything now," Michael said.

"Bet I'll hit more than you tomorrow."

"Do you really wanna bet?"

"No." (Roman had once lost fifty dollars to Michael on a bet that the current day of the week was, in fact, Thursday. It was Friday.) Michael sat back triumphantly.

The stars faded once more as they talked and drew nearer the lights of Lake Charles, crossing the river again, its dark waters colored faintly by the line of bright casinos down its bank. The sight revived memories of former evacuations in caravan with the Schiros, which journeys always devolved to pilgrimages in quest of the state's great buffets. For some minutes they spoke of steak and snow crab and the attendant with her vacuum at a short remove from Uncle Mark's seat.

They turned off of I-10 and meandered through darkening streets toward the shore of Lake Calcasieu, speculating on the hunt. After some slow miles peering for lanes which seemed now to take them into the marsh, they parked before a lodge set high on pilings above a canal cut from the lake.

"Man, it got cold," Roman said as they stepped onto the oyster shell road.

"Yeah, that's good--ought to push some more birds down."

At the swish of a seal the three looked up to see their hostess framed in the bright yellow light of the doorway above. From her inscrutable mouth came a Cajun trill: "Welcome, welcome, y'all come on up!" She waited, motionless, as they ascended the steep stair, and extended a slender hand to each in turn as they passed within, introducing herself as Annabel Lavender. She was a tall woman, thin but firmly curved, with short blonde hair that lifted in feathered waves from her tanned brow.

She led them through a den deep with leather couches and ringed with mounted ducks and geese and into a kitchen attached to a sunroom where stood a large round table. Through the wide windows, beyond the broad lake evidenced by the depth of its darkness, burned the fires of refineries.

"Y'all start on this while I finish the etoufee, alright," she said, placing before them a silver platter piled with cheeses, crackers, morsels of duck and deer sausage, and a variety of peppers. "The bar's all yours, too, Mr. Moran."

Roman, reluctant to sit, chewed a bit of duck as he edged around the kitchen walls studying the columns of framed photographs. In most men posed with heavy stringers of speckled trout and redfish or behind rows of mallards, teal, and geese laid out in neat, sumptuous rows. One or two featured a dolphin, apparently pink, sporting beside a white boat. Several others showed the marsh at dawn, the sky aflame and clouded with ducks by the thousands.

"Are they this thick all the time, Miss Lavender?"

She knew without looking what he meant. "Well, honey, not anymore. Most of those pictures are a little bit older than you are."

She bent over the table to lay out glasses and silverware and Roman glanced as her blouse fell away slightly from her neck to reveal the whiter skin below her shoulders. Then, stomach tightening as his father did the same, he turned his gaze again to the fires in the window. He hardly heard his father ask how the hunters had been doing lately.

"Limits most days. Today was slow, but things should pick up with this front coming down."

She sprinkled a handful of green onion over the etoufee and pronounced dinner ready. They ate rapidly, driven by hunger as much as by the need to save their tongues from the stew's intense spice. Glancing over from her tidying, she noticed how quickly they drained their water glasses.

"What's the matter, boys? Thought y'all's from New Orleans!"

After the etoufee came cold pecan pie. Thus sated, Roman, always fascinated by such things, strolled about the den inspecting each piece of taxidermy: the mallards' iridescent heads shifting as he moved from purple through blue to green; the blue-winged teals' crescent faces and blue moon necks; the Blue, Ross, and Canada Geese locked in descent to some imagined marsh.

As the next day would begin before four, the Morans retired soon after Annabel, framed one more in the door against the darkness to bid them luck, departed. For what seemed hours Roman lay awake on his bunk, motionless, excited as well as anxious for the chances of the hunt. He had hunted ducks just twice, and that a few years prior, and then he had only four shots and missed them all. His being grown now would help, but with stature came the pressure of success, and he knew no successful precedent.

When he did fall asleep, he dreamed again of the desert. He wandered for what felt days of constant light from dune to dune, his skin cracking, bleeding, burning, until he met an old man at the base of a cliff which rose, yellow, pink, and spotted with scrub, two hundred feet above the desert floor. The old man's cancerous hide almost shone with spots of age and bristled here and there with patches of coarse hair. He gestured to a cave in the cliff wall and fell forward into the sand, his haggard breath dying in the fine yellow grains.

Roman turned away from the brittle heap which seemed already blowing away on the rising wind and crept to the cave's mouth. A cool air coursed over him from within. He drank from a pool at the cave's end, trusting in the dull gleam of the now distant light that the water, if it was water, would be good. Its chill touch teased him and he lay in it for many minutes, delirious. When he came again to his senses he found a key in his hand and saw a stair at the other side of the pool, visible now to his acclimated eyes. He climbed through darkness, drying as he went, once or twice peering down intently, thinking he heard harsh breath, until he reached what felt like a wooden door. It opened by the adventitious key onto what seemed a bright city of white stucco buildings, its white stone streets lined with palms. He walked alone down the stones, though voices called strange temptations to him from dark, perfumed doorways and alleys vivid with color and music. And despite the variety of their offerings they all spoke the same words in siren chorus: "Ut deus, Ut deus, Ut deus."

At the end of the straight street there soared a palace of stone gilded in the now lowering Sun, its towers and domes dotted in gems fired with all conceivable color. The gate of the palace was a great mirror, and it was just as he caught sight of himself in its silver surface that he woke to the sound of his guide's low voice.

"Alright, y'all, gotta get up if we gonna kill any birds."

He flipped the light switch in the bunk room, and Roman woke in the shade of a half-desperate feeling, a sense of nearly having remembered something whose loss could scarce be conceived.

Struggling into jeans, boots, and camouflage jackets, they made their way to the kitchen where orange juice, biscuits, and eggs lay waiting. After eating quickly and quietly, double-checking that all of their gear was in order and loading it into the pickup, they followed their guide down dark, deserted streets toward the flooded rice fields where the ducks would come to feed.

"Those eggs were like the ones we used to make for you and mom," Michael mentioned as they drove.

"You mean they were bad?"

"What the crap, Dad, why would you say that!"

"Sorry, I don't know. It's early."

The stars were visible now, hard-looking in the cold air which had flowed over the rice fields in the night. They shone fiercely as though knowing they would soon be obscured, flashing through the mostly bare branches of the maple trees lining the slightly elevated road.

At last they parked beside a thick stand of maples dotted with oaks and pulled on their waders in the chilly dark. The waders were of cheap rubber and fit loosely if at all, hanging in sagging folds around the boys' thin chests and at first only heightening the chill as the cold material sucked at their skin. With guns cased and shells--two boxes each--in their backpacks, they climbed onto Chris's large ATV, which pushed steadily through the shallow fields and onto a slight island in which a comfortable, dry blind lay embedded, concealed by roseau cane. The stars had grown dim by the time Chris had checked the positioning of the decoys against the wind. One star hung straight ahead of Roman on the horizon when he returned.

"Alright, boys, load 'em up, but make sure safeties are on. Keep ya faces down when we got birds comin in. When I say 'kill 'em' y'all get up and let 'em have it. Don't move a muscle til then and most important, like I said, don't look up. Them birds see our big ol' moon pie faces and they gone."

He said all this quickly, happily, with a confidence which rendered slightly comic the boys' grave visages and Jack's groggy countenance and which communicated itself across the thin wooden bench on which they all sat. Thus instructed even the shotguns' thin black muzzles nosing through the cane seemed to brighten with the steadily approaching Sun.

Just as the Sun edged over the horizon, hardening the lines of cypresses in the east, Chris muttered, "Bird comin' in on the left." They waited, breath quickened, heads down. Roman, farthest right, did not expect to shoot and felt relief.

Suddenly Chris said, "Kill 'em!" and the three stood up as a mallard hen crossed behind the blind. Michael and Jack shot twice each, rapidly and wildly. Roman, who had spent hours imagining the moment, seeing himself as the last line of defense against grim hunger in the form of unscathed feathers fleeing on the wind, who had thought and thought and thought over what he must do, for once did not think. His hands swung the gun up smoothly, with the habit of hours on the clay pigeon range, mounted the cool stock against the cushioned contour of his shoulder and the curve of his cheek. His eyes had never left the bird and now took into account the iron bead at the end of the barrel, which swung steadily with the hen, pulling ahead of her just as she dipped into an awkward curve out past the end of the blind. Hands, eyes, brain all followed as the hammer fell, and then a sudden warmth coursed through the boy as he watched her crumple, the flight feathers guided only by their own form as she plummeted into the shallow water twenty yards away, hidden by a clump of grass. He had killed his first bird, had killed her even on a difficult shot, as the others affirmed in the excitement of the hunt's first flush. They hunted without a dog and so he would not feel the soft feathers in his shaking hand until later but he knew that he had killed and that he would eat the flesh he had taken.

Ten minutes later, calm restored and heightened by confident expectation, Chris whispered another bird's approach from the left. It was a massive mallard drake, his wings whistling in the force of his course, his head, fiercely extended, glinting purple in the fresh light. Roman had a shot again, and knowing he had shot well without effort the first time thought to replicate the effortlessness and in doing so shot far behind his mark. The mallard vanished, quacking his escape.

In the midst of renewed self-doubt advancing in the awful specter of solitary luck, Roman renewed his faith by downing a speckledbelly goose flying high over head. His first shot, as so often with geese in their deceptively ponderous flight, fell far behind, but he pumped and followed smoothly and fired again. This time the long wings folded and the mottled feathers fell with a crash not five yards from the blind. Roman would gaze on it throughout the rest of the hunt, amazed by its size, tracing the blood that snaked from its head through the still water.

"Ribeye of the sky!" Chris crowed.

The shooting continued regularly for the next two hours. A flock of Green-winged Teal buzzed like angry bees into the decoy spread, cupping their wings quickly and coasting to a chittering halt on the water's surface. Michael shot two of them as they jumped back up, realizing their mistake. One was an uncommonly handsome drake, a mature bird in full color, the green stripe light against his cinnamon head, his breast evenly spotted.

Then Jack shot a fine drake pintail, but as he swung on the hen his gun jammed. Hurriedly he examined it, trying by harsh jolts to rack the slide and dislodge the stuck shell when suddenly there burst from him: "Ahh this thing is ------ up."

Michael, staring out over the water, either heard nothing or ignored it or didn't care. Roman, on the other hand, felt again the bolt of nothing, stripped of use and comedy, and, heir to his mother's feeling, turned and stared, pale suddenly and wide-eyed. He had only ever heard his father curse on occasion, and each time it had seemed hollow, a posture to impress his friends or brothers.

"Dad," he whispered.

His father turned to him, the motion slow, pained; to his surprise, Roman saw something he could only interpret as shame rising in his eyes. He had not intended to guilt, and he wished now that he'd refrained.

They looked out over the fields, hoping for a sight to clear the air which hung suddenly heavy and close about them though the day, still cold, had grown bright and the wind had washed all traces of cloud from the hard blue sky.

"I'm sorry, Roman," his father whispered. Roman had heard his father say this, at least to him, almost as rarely as he had heard him curse, and the rarity did not escape him. Nonetheless he continued to feel, and he realized that the burden of the feeling lay mainly with him, that another stone he'd long thought unshakable had been shifted.

His shooting, to this point in the hunt much better than anticipated, now took a downward turn, though he hit one more goose in the only other shot, aside from the first, which remained clear in his memory. The bird had crossed the blind high over his head, the dark streaks of its belly clear now in the high morning, and Roman had fired at the zenith. The goose seemed at first unscathed, and then, as Roman's gun swung to follow up, it had appeared to stumble, wings stuttering until it plashed into the water about a hundred yards distant.

Michael, meanwhile, had continued to fire joyously and accurately, and he now downed a mallard drake to complete his limit. Chris then called the hunt, and the three stretched and walked around the small strip of land, looking out over the fields, fearful some large flock or rare specimen should pass them by. Chris wound back and forth among the canes, pulling the fallen birds from the water and letting out a whoop when he found Roman's second Specklebelly. He returned and laid the birds out on the ground of broken roseau, and Roman brightened as he studied their feathers, vivid in the

Sun, shining with the drops of water standing on their plumed backs. After a minute he turned to Chris: "Where's that first hen?"

"Sorry, bud, I couldn't find her. Sometimes these birds fall but they can still kick around. Might be a mile away by now."

It was the thought of that duck, wounded perhaps, paddling crippled through the canes toward strange death, which sparked in Roman the feeling of remorse he would come to know well in his years of hunting, the certain knowledge of having taken another creature's life. He would in later years think this pang a sign of proper sympathy and consider that the day he felt nothing would be the day to lay down his guns forever. At the time, though, he thought none of this. He had, of course, killed many fish, but there was always a sense of possibility attendant on setting the hook. The hook could always be removed. But the trigger bore its irrevocable burden. He could not return life to the crumpled wings, and it was at the moment but a small comfort to think that the life he had taken would be drawn into his own. He felt rather that he was drawn now into the blood spilled.

They clambered back onto the ATV, slightly heavier now with flesh and hollow bone. They churned through the blue-gold fields, Roman noticing in the canes a greater abundance of color, flower, and chorus than he had thought possible there. They came closer and closer to the lines of cypress and maple. In the pre-dawn gloom Roman had thought the branches all bare, but he saw now that a few leaves yet clung to the maples' arms and that these burned bright and crisp as blood.

"Chris, any good taxidermists between here and New Orleans?" Jack broke the tired silence that had risen among them.

"There's John Louvrier in Breaux Bridge. Does the best work I've seen. Gonna get that teal done?"

173

"Yeah, I thought we might get that and one of the geese."

"Ah, their wings are so messed up, man, I wouldn't do it."

Roman recognized in his father's inquiry a subtle attempt to suborn him. He had seen it several times before, as once when his father had timidly presented Michael with a baby rabbit as recompense for having yelled at him, which was in turn recompense for Michael's having (accidentally) broken a ceiling fan with a baseball bat. Readily he acquiesced to his father's overture. Again he mused in murky tones on the incongruous prodigality by which the last three months, which ought to have been among the worst in his life, had shaken him from the malaise of the way laid out for him. He knew nothing of his parents' finances, of what was whispered and argued in the conclave of their midnight anxiety, and he but dimly suspected the extent of his father's audacity and his mother's accomplishment.

For an hour again he sprawled across the back seat of the pickup truck, thinking of the bright birds arranged in the ice chest just behind him, signs plucked from the sky now speeding eastward on wings forever folded. Presently they came upon Breaux Bridge and after crossing the eponymous Pont into its central district of Cajun restaurants and antique shops, turned down a lane and, passing St. Bernard's brown brick facade, pulled up to a building of blue wood set back on a drive of white gravel. It had the look of a new construction, and the small maples and oaks scattered about the tidy grounds were still staked straight. Beside the door hung a small brass placard engraved:

Nature Mort Taxidermy
J.F. Louvrier, Proprietor

Roman turned the halting handle of the front door. A sudden dimness relieved the bright November sun without, and a bell chimed lightly as his pupils swelled. To the right of the doorway loomed a dark room, evidently of some size. Its one window let in a faint glow at the edges of its curtained compass, shrouding feathered forms within in a ghostly solidity.

Ahead there opened a long, narrow room, evidently a workshop. Beyond the door frame, out of view, there shone the revealing white light of a strong lamp. In its stark stare the dried and colorless skin of a long-speckled trout hung mounted on a plywood panel, waiting to be painted. From beyond the light swam a pair of large, square glasses, and behind them a pair of blue eyes, liquid and luminous. "Good day," came a deep voice, almost placeless in its rich tone, like that of a local radio personality never seen by his audience. As the voice sounded the large, lapidary face moved into the lamp light, and the glasses flashed opaque in the white glance. "John Louvrier, what can I do for you?" The large man, well-rounded and robust, now seemed to soar above the three Morans as well by his size as by a certain stony vitality.

"Well, we're just coming back from Lake Charles and wanted to leave a couple birds with you."

"Excellent, let's see."

Together they moved back into the sunlight and around the back of the truck. Roman's father propped open the ice chest, revealing, laid atop their less lovely confreres, the teal and one of the geese. With a deft and gentle hand the man immediately seized the drake teal and turned it in the sun, rapt.

"Oh, this is an exquisite bird. I haven't seen one this nice in twenty years."

The green crest and vanes and isosceletic speckling stood out in the splendor of expertise, and the Morans stared as grown children who've just heard their mother's jewelry appraised.

After a contemplative moment John turned to the goose. Noticing his diminished enthusiasm Jack said, "I know the wings aren't in great shape."

John raised it, studied the dark-banded breast critically, replied, "Well, ya gotta kill it if ya wanna mount it."

The blood that had been tickling Roman's throat dissipated.

"Come on back inside and have a look around while I get your paperwork together."

Stepping back within and laying the duck and goose on a workbench, he turned toward the still darkened room. Soft incandescent light fell from wells in the vaulted ceiling, and Roman saw that what he had taken for a single room was in fact a series of chambers joined by broad archways. He had been once to the Museum of Natural History in New York. It had little prepared him for the riot of life which now erupted around him. He saw, often without knowing their names, Eiders in their spectacles and Mergansers in their hoods, Ocellated Turkeys and spare Sage Grouse, Tundra Swans, Barnacle Geese, Cinnamon Teal. He nearly stumbled across the massive carapace of a snapping turtle, which in turn leaned upon an alligator's twelve-foot effigy. He wondered at red and black and white squirrels as large as terriers. Fist-thick furs hung in prodigal ease across the back of an otherwise inexplicable chair. Lobsters and King Crabs scuttled from brine-brown baskets. Bluegill large as dinner plates slid from plexiglass worked miraculously into water. Each swath of wall and floor had been decked in life, stilled in the moment of memory or of inspiration, and a kind of contemplative desire stole over Roman then, somewhere between avarice and aesthetic.

John returned, and as Roman gazed he became aware of a stream of commentary from the taxidermist's mouth, rich, almost decadent, and acutely attuned to detail. Phrases broke in on his marveling consciousness: "Yes, the Saturnidae...the stippling on the shell took a full day...never seen them in Alabama?..migratory habits are sublime..."

At last it was felt that they must go. As they turned to the door, John stepped into his workshop, asking, "Before you go, do you have any interest in moonshine?"

They looked back. In the large, practiced hands glowed as with an inner murky light a bottle of brown liquid. A grey-white smile slipped from the partially open mouth, and the lamplight glared in the great glasses again.

"If only I did," Jack said, and the door closed with its light chime, muted by its own glass.

The green truck eased onto the quiet, well-shaded street; as they turned a corner the Morans noticed a sign in the window of a shabby cinder block store advertising hot boudin. Realizing suddenly that they had not eaten since before dawn, Jack pulled into its ill-marked parking lot, handed Roman a bill, and told him to go in.

The scent of cooking unencumbered by the vegetable broke over Roman as he pushed through the glass door. At the counter he ordered a pound each of seafood and of pork boudin. The steaming intestinal links were drawn from great silver pots and wrapped in white paper. As he waited to pay Roman, gazing absently through the store's front window, saw a man approaching in a sweat, his steps abrupt, his head low and shoulders hunched. The door opened and now the man was standing beside Roman. Without preamble he accosted the cashier, whose back was yet turned. "-----, I'm tired a' you."

She whirled as if in anticipation, brandishing her silver tongs. "Get your ------- ass out of here or Imma call my husband!"

Cowed, the man slunk back toward the door, casting back at each step a violent but frightened glance, and disappeared.

Roman's hand shook slightly as he handed the woman his bill. She smiled at him and Roman saw for a moment how beautiful she might have been. "Nothing to worry bout from him, hon. You just enjoy your food."

Nonetheless his heart beat harshly for some minutes longer, and he sat distanced from the convivium his brother and father still shared until in the food in fact he found ease.

It was not the rice, meat, and spice alone which drew the heavy humors from him, though he had ever reveled in such things and to have them neatly packaged in intestine for one-handed consumption seemed to him one of the greater advances of culinary genius. His mind had moved into vague and vivid realms of memory and myth, to the thought of his father chauffeuring him and Michael slowly through oaks lit with blue and yellow stars, red and white canes, green dinosaurs glowing in the night, through gingerbread Christmas villages and past crowds drawn closer together in the cheerful cold. And when he had eaten he drifted into a dreamless doze.

vi

They reached home in the middle of the afternoon, the sun bright and wild in the still fierce wind. They laid the birds out on the porch, arranging them by size. Their mother eyed them nervously, wishing dearly they weren't on the porch and wondering if they might bear bird flu. Nonetheless she seemed happy.

"Did y'all have fun?" She knew nothing about fishing or hunting and practically never would through her long years of secondhand experience therewith; through them all, this remained the extent of her questioning.

Michael provided an animated account, pointing to each bird and detailing its death in chronological order. Again

Eloise felt that this was more than she would like to know, but she couldn't help laughing at Michael's exuberance. She bore suffering enough in her own soul and sought to draw back from what burden she could avoid, though she did so without seeming selfish.

Jack showed the boys how to press the feathers from the puckering papery skin of the birds' breasts, how to slice down and out along the bone to pluck the rich red meat, how to wash and cut so no trace of feather, fat, or blood remained. The teal he cut into bites which he wrapped in bacon and garnished with cheese or jalapeno and grilled. He sautéed the mallard in butter, pepper, soy sauce, and Worcestershire and added it to a pot of gumbo. Finally, he roasted the goose with mushrooms, onions, and garlic, adding the fat to a dark roux he whisked for nearly an hour, beer in one hand, spoon in the other. The only meat they would eat for the following week was thus plucked from the sky, though still Eloise refused to partake.

After dinner they pushed back some of the furniture in the living room and Roman and Michael examined every aspect of the morning's hunt and speculated as to when they might hunt again while Jack and Eloise danced to a big band album she'd found that morning. Roman and Michael had rarely seen their parents show much direct affection and found it in some measure awkward when they did, but this was different. Their mother seemed alive when she danced, and though both of the boys disliked her often cold temperament they both realized, perhaps barely at the level of consciousness, that it spread from some brokenness within her, some lack which had begun in her youth and had splintered as she aged. It was one of the boys' again barely conscious understandings, and one of their deepest fears, that this brokenness should form a staple of their inheritance.

An hour later, all of them tired, they dispersed to shower, to pray, to rest. Later still Roman lay in bed, trying to sleep, frozen to his bed yet feeling a burning in his head and his stomach urging him to move. The house sounded asleep, and he rose from the sheets, trembling a bit as he crept down the hall, through Michael's room, and slowly, slowly, down the iron spiral stair, turning right again, again. A lamp yet glowed, and he stopped, calmed for a moment, gazing at the lazuli birds that graced its shade and at the darker devices of the other lamps: a man and a woman, a whale, stars and moon, white glass and black. Then he pulled the lit lamp's chain and released it with a quiet but harsh clangor as of the devil's interval distilled. Trembling more he shuffled into the kitchen where the screen of the computer glowed softly in the dark. All his body heavy with heat, blood pounding in his ears, he clicked and typed and clicked and stared, listening urgently for any sign of approach.

After some minutes the creak of a floorboard beat the blood from his face. Almost in a panic he closed the screen, leaped up, and walked away, plainly guilty, into the living room. He noticed as he passed toward the stairs that the lamp chain he had touched swung gently, as if held for an inquisitive moment and then released.

VI.

NO FINE THING SINCE

In three months the twentieth year would end, and some time after midnight he and Patrick sat still talking in the hostel's dim common room six floors above the Naples street lined and stacked with trash of six weeks' strike. The chianti stood between them on the table's edge, most of it gone to Patrick since he yet felt little taste though he had eaten freely of the famous pizza he alone had conjured of his passable tongue.

He read a poem he'd composed a week before in Greece and which he thought so fine in the metric of his own design, snapping shut at the close of each stanza, for dimly he'd begun to see the need of law and the pain of posing one's own, but this he thought fine most for its beginning in the dark rocking on the Adriatic when he'd gone on deck in the grey dawn just as they crossed to the north of Ithaca. In Epidauros it was done, though later he would blush grateful the guards had stopped his reading, glad when he knew it not good, that it had captured his feeling though the feeling was wrong.

He'd been weary with the ruins and the eye for thieves in the dark streets, but now he felt his blood again as he looked at Patrick gazing back in silence nodding till at last he spoke without at first a word for the verses.

"Have I told you before about the dance?"

181

"No, I don't think so."

"Long ago I thought that all of us are moving in a dance in all directions like creatures in the sea, back and forth and up and down and in and out on currents imperceptible to all but the best. Some in permanent pairs; others drifting after years to see each other through the sea beyond the shoulders of the new. And you and I have danced for a long time now, perhaps almost as long as we have or a quarter at least, and our circuits have neared each other at last and each of us pushes part of our world into the other's, even part of our memory, so that if we stay near long enough I will no doubt tell you things to make me less but never forgotten.

"Someone skips a beat, and someone deafens and sinks into some black trench and vanishes, but most still live, I think, even once they've died, washed along like shells in slow surf. And God in bare feet picks us all up eventually, even the fragments, and shows us all somehow to advantage, and we hear the dance perfectly at last and listen in ecstatic stillness.

"Art can give the stillness. Perfect drama moving over and over, Monet's skylight canvases--have you ever noticed how everything depends on the Sun?--every good piece is like that--a window in the floor of Heaven to say some bit of analog is right.

"Anyway, I think you've hit on something here, though I don't have much to say."

"Thanks." He paused for a moment and they listened as two men shouted in the street below, whether in mirth or rage they couldn't tell. Flatulence erupted in the next room.

"There are some I was very close to who it seems I've lost, and yet they're closer to my mind all the time."

"Yes, I think that's often the way."

"What does that mean?"

"That we have to leave everything behind eventually, and that it can all be taken or all be given. But it all begins to play on our eternity."

They sat in silence then until the wine was gone and went to bed, though it was not until the first sounds of the new street had begun that he drifted into sleep.

i

Roman awoke irrevocably at five on the Monday after Thanksgiving. It was not his first awakening since he'd gone to bed, for his stomach had troubled him, and when he now rose and stumbled into the bathroom, he found his face wan, his eyelids dark, the eyes cracked by thin bands of blood. Nausea swept over him as he stood in the shower, and he considered asking to stay home. Slowly, though, he improved, and the cold air on the stairs invigorated him to the point of asking his mother for a cup of coffee. Surprised, she nevertheless obliged.

When Roman and his father stepped onto the porch at 5:30, a strong wind was moving through the oak in the driveway. Branches creaked as the cold air coursed in icy fingers through the grey curls of Spanish moss. The cold came wet that day, heavy and sharp, cutting through clothing, and Roman shivered on the seat of the truck as he waited for his father to start the engine. They bounced down the dirt drive in the dark, hardened in the night, balancing their mugs as well as they could. Occasionally a drop splashed onto Roman's dry hand and burned for a moment.

As they turned onto the road, Roman saw in the yellow streetlight a farmer leading out a cow into his field. Its white, impassive face gleamed dully as it plodded on in silence as if to the altar.

Darkness still held sway when they broke from the leaning precincts of the woods and joined the calm but steady stream of traffic toward the Causeway. They crossed the Bogue Falaya River, where Roman watched a small boat a moment as it beat its way downstream, its fore lights plowing as well as they could into the cold.

They passed through Covington and then Mandeville, the sum of the headlights slowly glowing about them until they funneled onto the Causeway and the car beams dissipated in the vast bowl all around. The Sun had not yet risen, but the east had taken on an aureate blush, and Roman saw in the West the spectroscopic study he had noticed before, the subtle sifting of colors from lavender through hues of green to the deep but brightening blue of the dawning sky.

Then the Sun broke the horizon, and with it the wind took on a livelier strength, urging on their progress and beating in the eyes of the pelicans and gulls who sailed just above and beside the bridge, riding the wind and the great current of the commute.

They reached Metairie, and here the artery into which all had been gathered broke off in capillaries, cars splitting off in all directions as Roman wondered at the variety of life all around, at the thought that some of these people, bound to him in the marathon of the bridge, would go now to high corner offices downtown, others to cafes in the Garden District, others to the shipyards, some to business, some to trysts, some to dice, all contributing their share of power, pleasure, and wisdom to the throbbing sum of human life. He thought of the sickness he had felt that night, of the lusts which rose so frequently within, and he wondered what sicknesses and lusts vitiated and advanced the crowd crawling to their appointments and projects. He felt that his life at Ignatius lay at once within and without this great exhaustion, that a taint of futility lingered on the taste of each test and essay.

It occurred to him then that however small a part postulates might play in the daily pattern of his future, there were elements of his time dramatized by the setting of the soul, and that there might then lie some existential panacea in the danger he believed surrounded Francis.

The brown bricks themselves had by this time risen from the oak trees into view, and the dreadful anticipation surfaced in Roman's thoughts once more. Here, he thought, was the last of the beginnings. They drove up Palmyra Avenue, where nearly all of the homes stood uninhabited, where all the doors bore the brown watermark and the official orange spray paint listings of people and animals found inside, those dead and those alive. Warnings to looters, too, often burst from stained facades in sprayed orange lettering, as on one two-story corner which proclaimed, "I WILL KILL YOU DEAD!"

As on that morning in August's end, Jack dropped his son off with a "Go get 'em, Rome," and Roman entered the courtyard by an iron gate, cold and creaking in the gelid air. Today, though, only a few students stood in the courtyard, these few huddled and hooded and moving slowly from foot to foot. Most of the boys thronged the hallways of the second, third, and fourth floors--the first still lay off limits save for the restrooms.

Wandering down the halls beneath the gazes of the trophies and champions and donors, Roman found Francis sitting across the way from the Math department under a photograph of one of the school's presidents, Fr. Byron James. With him sat a boy who, despite his small size, Roman recognized as a Senior. His skin was dark, his eyes large, with whites which seemed disproportionately so. Roman paused, looking down questioningly at his friend, who sat engrossed in conversation with this new acquaintance. At present Francis noticed Roman.

"Oh, hey, Rome--this is Spencer."

"Spencer Zazulak," said the newcomer, offering a smooth, firm hand.

"Roman Moran. You're one of the Euterpe editors, right?"

"Yes, I suppose so, though I assure you that rag would look much different were I given any real editorial clout. Are you a writer?"

"Not really. I've dabbled here and there."

"I thought I smelled duck. Who's your English teacher?"

"Pearce."

"Ah, the Pelican! What do you think of *The Merchant of Venice*?"

"I don't know. Better than *Romeo and Juliet*. We had to act that out last year at our old school. Francis was Romeo and I was Balthasar."

"Odd that you weren't Romeo, isn't it?"

"Our teacher said something about Francis and the troubadour spirit and whatever else..."

"If only Pearce had such a sense of the poetic."

"Hm?"

"Always he stops with who and what. The why and how are all there are."

"I don't see why it matters so much. It's all a memory game anyway."

"Precisely the point, my friend. It shouldn't be, and it matters everything. That's why you don't see."

Roman, not a little annoyed, began to respond but was cut off by the bell, at whose summons Spencer conveniently--so Roman thought--sauntered away.

"What's with him?" Roman asked, eyes fixed still on Spencer's retreating form.

"I don't know, that's just his way.."

"Mm."

"I didn't like him much at first either, but he's brilliant."

"How do you even know him?"

"Spanish--says he needs another tongue."

"Good for him."

And each went his way.

ii

The students expected a rousing speech from Fr. Muller that morning. At least, they expected to hear his voice; few anticipated arousal. This was a new morning, and it must be marked by the usual custom. No exhortations to virtue came, though, and the morning announcements were read in bland and stumbling tones by some student who, conscious of the slight squeak in his voice, pitched it unrecognizably low.

Fr. Muller was in fact at that time meeting with his administrative team, several of whom had suggested that he fire those of the faculty still absent from the New Orleans area. He staunchly refused, and the meeting ended in grumbling and shuffling of sulky feet as all but one of the board slouched off to vent his frustration on an unsuspecting underling.

Only LaCour, one of Muller's oldest friends and an Ignatius Prep classmate, remained behind in the office on the third floor. He had gained a good deal of weight--a function of his nerves--in the weeks since Houston, and he shifted it now from one aching foot to the other. As he waited for his friend to speak, he looked through the window at a young hawk perched in the oak outside, studying its striated brown-black coloration until the door closed with a slight, familiar squeak and groan.

The two looked at each other for a moment, half-smiling. Then Muller moved to the window and stood, hunched and gazing. "I assume you wonder at my display?"

"Questions have occurred."

"Well, really it's quite simple. I signed the contracts. None of the board did."

"Yes, contracts they've violated by not doing their jobs. Besides, I've never known you to be a strict legalist."

"There's never been a time like this."

Stephen looked at his friend, a slightly strained cast to his mouth. Muller sighed, the only concession he would grant his weariness, looked briefly through the window at the hawk, flapping its wings for balance, and then turned his gaze to the crucifix above the window frame. At last, gazing again without, he asked, "Did you know that all of this used to belong to the society?"

Behind him Stephen said nothing. He felt a chastening had begun.

"Everything from here to the river, just about. I think about them all the time, coming down out of Acadia into this swamp and the fevers and the heat, building something on the government's gift. And the novices were in the wet fields with the slaves I'm assured were treated well, as far as slavery goes. And altogether they watched the life and death of the year and the green indolent growth and the red-eyed reaping and the moon rolling up and down the river. Then the repression and the land's exchange and purchase and restitution. And just last week the lawyers came and said the claim is ours and now would be the time to act. But I'm the one who's meant to be a slave, and those novices at the gins.

"God knows I've spoken in his cause enough in this job and I've heard his whisper all the time that he has no causes and causes are the enemy and that it was in the great cause that the serpent stretched his tongue to Eve. And now the cause is the school and the school for Christ who now needs the money we're paying people far away because of their homes or spouses or children or just because they're afraid to come back to Carthage. And for once I have the chance to give."

He fell silent then and turned the half-smile of self-mockery to Stephen, himself now smiling as well at the rare familiar flame.

"That collar's made ya a real pain, ya know that?"

"You've followed me in worse."

They looked at each other a moment longer, aware, in a whisper in the backs of their minds, of their friendship's fragility. Then Stephen turned, opened the blank white door of the office, and strode off down the dark wood of the hallway. Muller allowed himself ten seconds' reverie and then returned to his desk, signing countless letters as the hawk behind him called.

iii

Meanwhile the first classes of the day had begun, and as students settled into the scarred, familiar desks displaced a bit by the scent of mold filtering up from the surrounding city, Spencer Zazulak stood in the bathroom, staring at the blank space which once had been his canvas, the four-year glory of the crap house poet. He should, of course, have been in class himself then, but time had set him on good terms with his Physics teacher, Mrs. Taggart; he thus found himself in sad possession of a few moments to contemplate his work's negation without the bother of the hobbledehoy.

All the stalls had been replaced, four years' slavery to the artistic spirit destroyed. Spencer could bear no grudge, though. He viewed himself as a mere intension of nature, and if nature rose up and effaced his designs, he must submit to design itself.

Nor could he be daunted. Hemingway once lost the manuscripts; what of it? He would sublimate the loss and trust that nature had multiplied his powers in the months since his studio's submergence.

Nonetheless, he found he had nothing to write at the moment, and anyone observing him closely as he returned to class would have found evidence of tears written in the smooth surface of his skin.

iv

A difference of vision such as arose between Francis and Roman that morning would have left Roman distraught in August. By November's end, though, he had formed new friendships and, almost against his will, begun to enjoy some of his classes, with the result that by the time Scripture arrived, just before lunch, he found himself once more in good temper. He noted the same restoration in Francis's face as they met at the door, and each sat with relief in his customary place at the back of the room, Francis just behind Roman. They had found this arrangement suited them, as it prevented them from distracting each other entirely. As Ruggi took a lax view regarding classroom management, though, they were free to speak as much as they pleased.

They sat quietly, happy in each other's company, as their classmates filed in and milled about, unafraid now of any real reproof should they be seen unseated once class began. John Delmonaco, a large boy of shapeless figure, pulled a slim volume of Greek and Roman erotica from Ruggi's cabinet, flipped to a page featuring a massive phallus, and held it at a perpendicular to his crotch. He stood then in triumph at the front of the class, first displaying his new and ancient appendage for the benefit of his peers and then turning and calling, "Hey, Ruggi!" The latter hurled an admonitory Greek dictionary and chased the thus castrate John to his seat amid a swarm of imprecations.

Class began, and Ruggi launched into a presentation of the story of Elijah and the prophets of Baal. It was a story which would later swell in Roman's imagination, and though he here and there caught an image of Elijah's confident taunts and the prophets' bleeding rage, he grew more and more uneasy, withdrawn, as a question rose over and over to the surface of his mind, bobbing like the corpse of a filleted fish. He felt it brooding just behind him, and he sought to suppress it, to focus on what lay before him, yet its whispered urgency increased in whines of lust and jealousy and anger at the possibilities it suggested.

At last he turned around, and the nagging tones in his head grew silent as he looked steadily at Francis and said, "Hey, are you still doing the whole agnostic thing?" Their eyes were fixed, and Roman saw that Francis's had assumed a pale green tone in the light of the classroom projector.

The answer came so quickly that Roman could only suppose later that Francis's thoughts, moving silently along across the chasm deepening between them, had kept pace with his own, or that at least he had desperately desired to speak it for some time now: "I'm an atheist."

"Oh."

Roman felt the exhaled word closing around him like his own lips, or like the lips of something far greater than himself just gripping him, lightly, moistly, almost lovingly, as in a delicate but supremely violent kiss. It was the speech of one at the click of the mine or the first creak of a wife's infidelity, and he turned away as quickly as decorum allowed, for the moment at least utterly vanquished.

A cold gripped him as he felt his friend drifting away behind him, and he drifted, too, in a darkness unshaped by stars, and colder lights shone in, or seemed to shine, on his mind, and chief among them, hard and bright, was the thought that he had failed or, more precisely, that he had been found wanting.

The lights came on again at noon, and Roman sat quietly gathering his belongings as his classmates filed out, chattering happily, excited by the prospect of food. Francis pushed against the current of khaki to the podium, and Roman watched as he spoke to Ruggi for a minute or two which felt indefinitely longer, unable to hear what they said for the thunder of hungry feet in the hall and possessed of the sense that he was not meant to hear. Feeling suddenly pettish he went on alone.

In the chill, bright courtyard he joined a group of boys he'd come already to know quite well. They were, for the most part, quiet, studious, and cordial, ready with but not solicitous about conversation, and they allowed Roman his silence.

Upon this brooding there broke waves of laughter issuing from a trio of young teachers some twenty feet to Roman's right. He had from his first days at Ignatius noted their sort with some interest, not only for their youth--none of his prior teachers had been younger than thirty--but also for a certain air of the dandy, an almost feminine aestheticism disconcerting at first but slowly growing more attractive. They wore linen in the warm months and Merino wool in winter, oxfords and tailored suits and a variety of color verging almost on plumage.

One of them, an English teacher, slight, well-built, and with a shock of hair swept conscientiously back in the style of the 20s, presently continued his entertainment.

"So he was telling me (and here his voice changed, evidently in imitation, to a tone at once high-pitched and deep, with an intensity of inflection almost oriental), 'Well, Michael, this year I'm going to Russia. There's a village right on the inside a' Siberia where there's a bar where there's a famous bottle of vodka with a man's toe inside of it. And I'm gonna drink that bottle right down to the toe. And ya know what ya gotta do when ya get to the toe?' What's that, Jimmy? 'Ya gotta suck the liquor out.' You gonna do it, Jimmy? And he just looked at me."

The others had with difficulty withheld their laughter during the telling; now there burst forth sharp reports of mirth, all three of them turning away for a moment, almost stumbling with spirit, and slowly returning to their triumvirate circle with labored breath and eyes wet at the corners.

Roman had observed many such prandial proceedings, and now as ever he felt in their words a lightening. He began, in consequence or not, to grow restless and thinking to soothe himself, crossed the courtyard toward the small chapel. As he approached the usual entrance he noticed, tucked between a stand of holly trees and a white stone statue of St. Ignatius, a door he'd not before seen. Curious, he touched the handle. It turned, and he found himself at the foot of a wooden spiral stair. On any other day he should perhaps have turned back, yet a strange incaution urged him upward, the blood loud in his ears. At the spiral's end he found himself in a confessional which he guessed to be just beside the altar. He supposed the chapel unoccupied, supposed, too, that his mode of entry was, strictly speaking, forbidden; accordingly, he cracked the door enough not to be seen and studied the noonday stained light. The pews appeared empty, and he slipped over the altar and into an antique wooden seat which creaked in well-worn sequence as he sat.

He had never sat so far forward before and thus had never seen the windows directly to his right and left. On his right against a porphyry sky spread a tree as if of horn, spindle-tined and bare of any growth. A violet water pooled about its roots, and in its many-forked branches perched an owl, an egret, and uppermost, a kingfisher.

To his left, too, stood a tree. Here the sky burned ruby, as if about to consume the radiant pear tree in its midst. Its limbs reached through long upward arcs, laden with white blossoms and fresh leaves. In the crook of its lavish embrace stood a pelican, beak to its breast, down which ran a spreading stream of lye-white blood. At the tree's foot stood a trio of sheep, their eyes upon the blood, the bole, and the bird.

The sun was high and each image caught it equally, and Roman looked a few times right to left and back again until finally in their passage his eyes caught at the center, and feeling himself formulated he found he must again move. He rose, hurriedly genuflected, and passed out into the administrative wing. In each direction, in and out of every door, swam faces blank with his obsession. His eyes could not define them, though he sensed their gazes, kind or questioning or set in some absent concern.

He reached the main corridor and rose by a green stairwell to the third floor, where he meant to cross to his locker by a balcony. Stepping into the deserted, bracing air, he paused, and resting his forearms on the thick round railing, observed the mass of his classmates fifty feet below. As he gazed a heavy tingling began in his calves and grew through his stomach toward his heart. He had forgotten the strength of the urge to fall and now it turned to him unmasked. There was no question of desire or despair but simply the command of a forgotten voice returning from the bottom of time. With a sudden movement, as a flick of the wrist or tightening of the jaw, he turned back through the swinging doors into the growing grumble of students, and the voice died away.

As he neared his locker, he came upon the Scripture classroom and with a sudden tightening of the bowels watched Francis emerge, his face flushed with something like the shadow of triumph. Turning, Francis saw him, and the two stopped some paces apart.

"You been in there the whole time?"

"Mhm."

"What did you talk about?" Roman did not want to ask, but a sickening need, a desire to look down from the wall at the corpses outside, urged him on.

"God."

"What does he think?"

Francis looked back at him, eyes inscrutable and superb. "I've told you already."

The silence resumed--not the comfortable sort they had always known, but one filled with discordant voices. They began to walk, still some feet apart, but level. At last Roman, perhaps shoved over the edge of some precipice by the maddening--seemingly impossible, even--lack of concern Ruggi showed, spoke his utmost concern. He sensed that he overplayed his hand, whatever hand he might have, yet as the situation had precipitated so swiftly, and as he sensed, too, that this confrontation would be the only one of its kind, he wished nothing more than to get to the end of the matter.

"Don't you want there to be God?"

"Why should I?"

"Isn't it a better world if God exists?"

"Is it?" They paused in front of a window looking out over the city toward the Garden District. Francis's pale skin flashed pink in the high sunlight. He stared as if sick on the neighborhood. "Look, Rome." Roman looked out on the sea of abandoned houses, the water line plainly visible as if the rough animal had slouched along begging a scratch of every surface. The pink brilliance of the rain trees' blossoms had begun to pale in the recent cold, the form of all faded bouquets floating against the sky. Dead trees everywhere raised their grey knuckles against the light. "All ashes, no God hiding in the fire. Isn't ash what you believe in anyway?"

Roman paused for a moment and glanced back at Francis, still squinting at the trees, his thick eyebrows nearly touching.

"No. But if you think that, why wouldn't you want something better?"

The longest pause followed here, as if Francis weighed everything he said, unsure wherein lay the best saying. At last he spoke.

"All I want's a way out."

The bell intoned its inviolable command, and Francis, with a look almost of pity, turned away, leaving Roman staring into nothing over the courtyard. A flock of pigeons rose from the roof in wheeling applause, while in their shadows the boys glanced up in quiet discomfort. And Roman walked away into the brightened and vanishing world.

v

When the bell rang at three that afternoon, Roman felt that its shrill voice shoved him into time once more. The two hours previous had passed insensibly--Latin, Biology resolved to indiscriminate background against which memory projected the dark enlightenments of the morning, seeming both to stretch him into dessicate eternity and to chain him to the livid moment.

He remained nonetheless impassive to space and shape, passing entranced and deaf through the crowd of boys bustling languidly toward lockers and exits, spilling life into the dead neighborhood around. Roman's mind had fixed on one person, had begun to play out the encounter with him, passing through the possibilities of the exchange until it almost surprised him when, gazing through the door into the Scripture class, he found that the old man, shuffling papers, eyes fixed on his own purple-veined and papery hands, exactly matched the conception his brain had built.

He had nearly crossed the threshold when a familiar accent called to him, "Moran! Got a minute?"

Had his vision of the afternoon allowed for any interruption he should surely have said that he didn't and continued on his baleful way. As it was he struggled a moment in the doorway and then, snared between regret and relief, stepped toward LaCour, his face declining slightly to the left, his eyes dull with thought.

"Come with me, just a second," LaCour said, turning toward a peach-painted stairwell. Though LaCour had returned to New Orleans at the same time as the Morans, Roman had not been assigned to his classes. Their occasional conversations remained cordial, even warm, but now Roman knew not what to expect. His mind wandered over vague possibilities as he counted the thirty-two steps down, studiously if subconsciously avoiding the places where the ceramic paving squares had been chipped to bare concrete.

On the second floor the two turned briefly down a hallway bronzed with deep autumn in windows rising nearly to the ceiling. Again they turned right, now onto a narrow, somewhat shabby hall, and again right into LaCour's office. Three of its walls, and the fourth excepting the door, were lined in books, mostly British in authorship. From a high sill above an aged computer gazed a curiously impassive bust of Poe.

Seating himself in a well-worn swivel chair and bidding Roman take a scratched wooden seat, LaCour laid his hand on a slim volume atop his desk, and turning a highly-tuned bright eye to Roman, said, "You remember our first class together?"

"'Let be be finale of seem'," Roman responded. He had intended sarcasm, yet he found as the words emerged that they gained an impressive quality he should not have known how to convey. He calmed slightly.

"For whatever reason I keep thinking about that day and thinking you should have this." Sliding the book beneath his hand to the edge of the desk, he took it up and with a lively motion tendered it to Roman.

It was a simple volume, a white paperback imprinted with the single word "Harmonium" in azure letters.

Roman gazed somewhat dully down on it, impressed by the gravity of the gift, yet... "Why should I have it?"

"You could say I want you to make something. Ya ever try to make anything?"

In earliest boyhood Roman had made many things, mostly pictures of sharks and dinosaurs. He had thought them quite good when he made them, perhaps because he knew about the subjects: the number of slits in the Great White's gill flaps, the curve of a Tyrannosaur's tooth. Yet he had made but badly, and since then hardly at all.

"Almost every time I see you, you're sittin there thinkin. Eventually I think ya oughtta try to make something."

Whether from the frustration of his earlier project or in some despair at the thought of his own influence, Roman wavered for a moment on the edge of a confession. He felt suddenly the loneliness of the last months and wondered if in the room at that instant there existed just so much distance and intimacy as would allow him to unburden himself without fear of reproach.

For a moment he thought. Then he rose, said thank you and that he would read the book, and turned away.

Forty-five minutes yet remained until Roman's father would retrieve him, so he sat in the courtyard where the cold air had at least grown still and light and watched as the sea of students flowed out of its brown brick reef. It consoled him to watch his classmates go, to see their faces flowing with all manner of mood. They were in many ways a homogeneous bunch; they did not, at any rate, represent outwardly the diversity of their city. Yet Roman in his brief friendship with them had found them party and prey to all the race of beauty and of sin. Here passed one whose father had, just days before, hanged himself at the lake front. Here another went to revel in his calculus. All of them knew joy, and all of them knew death, and all of them already had enriched Roman immeasurably.

Once the yard had grown quiet he walked to the restroom; he had known the Causeway's toll on the bladder and wished to avoid it in future.

He stood at the sink for some time, pushing the timed faucet again and again, examining his reflection. His nose, grown recently more aquiline, distressed him, as did his increasingly thick eyebrows. More than at its excesses, though, he wondered today at the face's deficiencies. He could not place them, but he felt especially his inadequacies and wondered if they might not manifest in physiognomy.

His investigation faltered at the sound of soft footfalls, and looking deeper into the mirror he saw, with a rush of dislike, the form of Spencer Zazulak. He turned slowly, reluctantly, to meet him.

Spencer took him in with a slightly proprietary air and, raising a dark, thin eyebrow, wondered that Roman shouldn't have gone home by now, especially since he had seen Francis leave some time ago.

"It's not like we're joined at the hip or anything."

"You should hear him talk about you. But you grew up near each other, right?"

"Yes, in Lakeview."

"I lost a great deal, too," he said, glancing idly at the old stall. "But it seems to me that Francis has lost most of all, don't you agree?"

"What do you mean?"

"He's broken through the rind."

Roman stared at him.

"Surely our friend Ruggi's used the expression--breaking through the outer rind of life to get to the sweet fruit of reality. But I think it's really the other way around. It's more like we're inside the orange, one of all those little seeds sleeping in the sweet, juicy fruit. There are two ways out--either something on the outside breaks the peel, chews us up, and spits us back or swallows, or we simply realize we don't have to be a seed-- we can be a little worm instead--and chew our way out. Francis is out, and who knows whether anything at all is there, but perhaps some day we can help you escape, too."

He had taken three steps toward Roman and here laid a sympathetic hand on his shoulder. Roman felt its chill through his uniform, and his face reddened at the sudden thought that this stranger had penetrated Francis's interior life while he remained without, at the thought of Francis, Spencer, Ruggi, and who could say who else attending some cosmic conspiracy which left him alone in the cold light of belief.

And then, suddenly and without intimation so that he surprised even himself, he punched Spencer hard in the stomach. It was the first time he had done such a thing, and, fear rushing over him, he stretched out as if to catch his foe, stumbling, falling, head nearly knocking against a urinal. The shock which first registered on Spencer's face morphed shortly into an odd smile, and Roman turned away. But before he could escape, he heard the strained voice calling after him, weakened but gleeful: "You see! We've begun!"

And having nothing else to do--indeed, having come that afternoon expressly for the purpose, Spencer Zazulak hobbled to his stall to perfect his pain. Twenty minutes later he departed in bruised ecstasy, leaving behind what he thought was his supreme work to date, unblemished by the thousands of lines of verse less stellar.

Fire and Ice

Wish to love and hate's desire
free we worms from fruit's sweet fire
that caves and bellows in the gut,
feeding feral memory's glut.
And when the cells have split their sides,
spilling in the chilling ides,
the dogs will lick the killing floor
and life leak from the swollen sore.

His new career had begun, his life punctuated now by the only act of physical aggression he would ever encounter, his insight into the human condition sharpened incalculably by suffering.

vi

After as brief an exchange of pleasantry and inquiry as possibly with his father, Roman closed his eyes and cushioned his face on his seatbelt. He wished at first only to avoid any talk that might goad him into confession, as well, perhaps, as to ponder the day's events in order to compose himself for the sure scrutiny of the dinner table (there would be duck gumbo tonight and how a small part of him, undisturbed by the spirit's wild winds, wished to eat that meal composedly.)

His first thought, conjuring images from his lavatorial assault, put what composure he'd momentarily regained to flight, and had his father, disregarding the road, seen his son's face, he should have observed there a darkness and a furrowing and a frown to tell a long portion of the tale.

Senior, though, himself so slight. And suspect couplets crowding corridors blonde in Civics ducked to desk to grade and all the peering conspirators snickering so many footmen holding coats himself catching breath catching himself

201

seminal blood beating the archangel defend the death of exit. The dreamless night against eternity. No exit but no exit from the second problem and prime.

They were on the Causeway now, and the Sun was setting to their left, and the wind and the waves pushed toward the sun as if following the day around the world, and the crests of fierce, cold foam caught flame in their falling, and the gulls laughed high into the opalescent evening. And the sound of the white laughter and its memory soared in high melody above the rickety rhythm of the shocks along the sections of the bridge.

He slept dreamlessly until the darkness in which he'd departed that morning welcomed him again to the red dirt drive, dark in the yellow lights of the porch below the oaks. Once more he saw the face of the neighbor's cow, its whiteness turned full upon him now. As he stepped still sleepily from the truck a wave of dizziness passed over him. His brain, imbalanced by the bowing sleep along his seatbelt, found itself insusceptible of correction, and Roman, after mechanically kissing his mother hello, crept off to bed under cover of the general clamor of greeting. His mother, going to summon him to dinner, found him as if dozing, the lamp yellowing the fetal curve of his back, the vertebrae just visible below his shirt. She turned the lamp off and crept quietly downstairs, and Roman breathed more easily and soon fell asleep.

VII.

ONLY THE LOVER SINGS

And then in fact they woke him, as he'd expected when, home from comforting his cousin, he'd asked to be wakened should she change in the night. And near three they came, and he seemed already rising with the sudden light, as if the mind had charged the body with its stern anticipation.

And then in the car that soon would pass to him, flying through the park in the slight easing of the air below the oaks, his father's every art at work to reach the Mother, alone in her brick house barred at the windows in an earlier age.

Inside now, waking, calming, asking what medicine she needed and she in a low voice knowing all moaning, "Oh God, oh God," begging for it not to come too quickly.

And then again in the car, laws in abeyance, knocking on the aunt's door, and he now twenty, officious with exhilaration, drawing water for the old one's pill, and the joking uncle grim and the aunt rushing about like the mother in miniature, unable to breathe with the swift, higher exhalations, almost whines, "Oh God oh God oh God oh God" as if on the verge of vomiting.

Five now in the car in the final flight past the blind patrols to the hospital doors opaque with July's wet breath, and out of the car, helping the Mother racing eternity to the room and he rushing ahead, holding the doors until the dyed brown hair had hobbled in between her blood to rise to the seventh floor, the gears impervious to worry, the seventh where his mother had lain when the blood burst in her brain, and she, his mother, in time's sudden summoning its father now most calm.

The rest were in the room, the last of those there, and she most of all there, so different from the purple gown of two days prior, now lying limply rigid in the bed, the corners of the mouth turned down in sudden sharp ascent of the thirty-hour coma when they said she still could hear, and the anger of her betrayal which had burned so bald in light of their love dissolved and he whispered only the old love and the promise of pride, feeling his petty hope and fearing perhaps unknown to force forgiveness on the dying mind and rouse some reproof, hardening the soul in passage to its vast evaluation.

All said all drew back and his mother began the prayer all joined and then the uncle said, "That's all," and the awful beauty seized him and he stood breathless, staring, feeling he should be swept on, too, and wondering that they all somehow resisted the final presence in the room.

And then the wailing began, continuing in the hall until the grey coronation of the sun and he, in his officious youth as well, perhaps, as in some secret store engendered by his mother, became one of the comforters as slowly they tore themselves away, gathering again near the elevator and then again at the Mother's house where they would spend the several weeks while flowers heaped themselves dying in the den and the kitchen and the halls along with endless condolences and inquiries until the phone was disconnected, and in all she lay where she had lain most of the ten years prior in the leather chair before the blank TV while the space where her womb had been throbbed.

And he with her friend who flew the French flag that fourteenth day began the choice of words at which a fear of Lazarus, writhing from his cave, arose.

The day swelled and he began to sense its weight despite the surge as of the summer weekend at the sea, and he lay down, feeling as if he'd swum all day, on the couch alone in the living room where she had spent her purple afternoons between the grand piano and the stair, and his wife called him, though neither suspected, could have conceived even, that she would be his wife.

And the funeral came, warm in the church of cool glass and frescoed domes overwhelmed with July and with the endless stream of bodies creating in her wake a current toward the altar and it was in this current for the first time in nearly two years that he met Francis, and embraced him, and the scent that hung in his hair which was now long and wild touched his memory in which he and she in the casket fit so firmly.

Then he and the seven cousins bore the coffin to its car and followed in the limousine, sweating in suits as they turned into the grey plane of the graveyard, shadowless save for the copper tines of the stag's horns green by the sea, and they wound down the lanes of graves like little grey homes, tenants stacked like leaves raked up in fall, and the sun beat down so differently there than in the English cemetery that spring, fanned with cypress censers shaded by umbrella pines against the pyramid's pitiless gaze.

Once more they bore the pall and slid it through the grey and gaping mouth, and then at last he wept as he had done once the day he realized she would die, and his aunt, inconsolable the day it began, held him now as he had held her and looked at him and said as he wept that they would be ok, he the child once more now that nothing more could be performed.

i

When Roman had not appeared at the expected time, his mother, climbing the smooth wooden stairs, had found him lying stiff, wan, haggard in the relit lamp. It was plain he would stay home that day, though when she asked what was wrong he replied only that he hadn't been able to sleep.

She checked on him once more before leaving for work and found him in much the same state, with perhaps a touch more color in his face. She asked if he wanted to see the doctor; he did not, and as he didn't seem particularly ill she decided she could leave him for the day without incurring any charge of negligence.

He lay and listened to her steps on the stair, her tread heavy with weight gained in recent weeks, the noise of her egress growing as she clattered to the kitchen to retrieve her coat and keys and then ran across the porch to evade the cold. The engine fired heavily and the tires ground steadily up to the road, and Roman lay still listening for some moments to the oak twigs tapping the aluminum roof in the chill wind.

These tappings seemed full of some intent, relaying to him some inscrutable message from all of nature bent in to observe him. He had dreamed in the night of Francis as he had last seen him the previous day, staring with strained eyes out of a window onto the world, but he, Roman, was the world, pungent with wilting flowers, and he felt as if Francis searched him for some sign, some promising remnant to redeem the homes grown over in mold. He had watched through the glass as Francis spoke, found the mouth's motions foreign. And Francis had beat his palm against the glass, and he felt each fall as on a bright new bruise, felt it in a dull sensation which reached him everywhere without revealing anything, and he wondered if in all he saw this reveresque Francis took courage and confirmation. He did not know what Francis meant.

At length he rose, walked downstairs, his feet, slightly damp with sweating beneath the wool blanket, now clammy and cold on the wood floors, and poured himself a bowl of cereal. As he ate he gazed through the kitchen windows at the neighbors' great black dog frisking in the cold, nipping at the passing chickens and then pausing to scratch himself behind the ear with furious satisfaction.

He finished his cereal, tipped the bowl back to his lips to sip the sweet dregs of milk, and then stared for some time as the final lactic film, invisible above the bowl's white bottom, congealed, fossilizing on an infinitesimal scale the remnant bits of wheat and rice.

Once more at length he discovered he must do something or risk falling back at the breast of his forlorn and darkly muttering muse. He glanced around, saw the computer, felt none of the hot flash of its possibility, not on that day. His eyes lit on, took courage from, a photograph on the refrigerator of him and Michael after their recent hunt, fists full of birds' necks. He rose, studied it for some minutes, and then turned to the living room, where he and Michael had spent no small part of their time the past weekend at darts and pool. Addressing first the board, he was dismayed to find that his throws, at first, flew exactly to the point of aim. Prior to then he had reliably pushed his throws to the right and found that only misdirections made the mark. Now, though, as he adjusted to this newfound alignment of eye and hand, the darts began to fly as if at random, until finally one stuck in the wall.

He turned next to the pool table. Michael here had the mastery and now, without him here to see the tribute, Roman tried adopting some of his techniques. They did nothing to improve his shots, though, and he soon grew lax in lieu of opposition, cheated, stole shots from himself, until at last the air grew rank with frustration at his weakness and at the balls' intractability, and he thought to walk out to the street to check the mail.

Still in his blue sweatpants and grey shirt, his socks still sticky and stale, he slipped into sneakers and pulled on a brown fleece and stepped out into the cold, shaded air of the blue porch, careful to neglect his habit of locking the door behind him. The sun had come near its zenith, and it cast a shadow all around the great oak tree in the drive, and the dead leaves, which left the tree without removing any of its fullness, had fallen by the sure guidance of their forms on the breeze into the pattern of the shadow so that there seemed to Roman to be two trees there, one the fallen image of itself.

The air warmed slightly as he passed through the roving reticulum of light below the oak and then warmed more again as he stepped into the full sun on the red dirt drive flecked with yellowed stones. On his left a Kingfisher chittered into skimming view above the pond, snatching up a shiner rising into the shallows' warmth. On his right a yellowish horse stamped and snorted, his breath no longer vivid on the air. High above and beyond the horse a flight of ducks, mallards by his best guess, drove on toward the South on the strong wind. He had heard that they could travel eight hundred miles with a good wind and wondered where their day had begun and where the dusk might find them. Then he reached the pines that narrowed like jetties to the bay's mouth of the road, and his step quickened in the quickened cold and he pulled the sheaf of envelopes from the chill aluminum mailbox and hurried back to examine it in the light.

He slowed his pace again in the Sun and leafed through the letters, his dry hands caressing the smooth, cool paper, his head growing slightly dizzy as he continued to walk while studying the addresses, all unimportant to him to the point of meaninglessness until he came to a slim missive marked in Molly's elliptical hand. Here his heart jumped a bit and a touch of color came into his cheeks even in the sun. Suddenly he imagined her standing, as if across a ballroom, in a long dress of dark blue. He hurried back to the house, taking the steps at a run. The air inside seemed close to him now, and though not quite as yet sweating he felt stickily warm and so stripped down to boxers and undershirt and stood in one of the cooler corners of the den as he pulled Molly's marbled epistle from its envelope and read:

Dearest Roman,

Christ's peace be with you! I hope you had a beautiful Thanksgiving. I must say your preview of the menu sounded more than a little intimidating, if not gluttonous, though I suppose you might still meet the mean given the festival context.

We visited Daddy in Rome during the first part of our holiday. You would love the campus--vineyards and olive groves teeming with hedgehogs and the occasional wild boar; an ancient well once used by Saints Peter and Paul; pink walls that gather up the mellow sun streaming off the waves of the Tyrrhenian, cutting through the smoke of vine branch fires; the scent of wisteria hanging everywhere. It's all at the foot of Mount Albano, an ancient volcano turned gorgeous blue crater lake. We went up to the summit one day to visit Castel Gandalfo, the pope's summer residence. They keep the Vatican Observatory there (there's another one in Arizona, too). Daddy's friends with one of the astrophysicists, Fr. Blue. We met him at a giant wooden gate in the city, then he drove us up the mountain through Domitian's gardens--very Grecian to me, marble peering through the olives and such. Then he showed us the library and the telescopes and took us to the roof where we watched the swallows wheeling way up over the lake.

Then, of course, there's Rome itself. The difference of time scale always stuns me. In America we think something from the 1800s is old (which, of course, it is--ten percent of the way to Jesus), but this time we visited a temple dedicated to Jupiter dating back to 700 BC. Our family's more interested in the religious sites, obviously: St. Peter's Basilica (did you know it's big enough to hold any other church in the world?), where Peter's bones lie in the crypt and where his chair is kept and where you can see the circle of porphyry where Charlemagne was crowned; Santa Maria Maggiore, where they keep the gilded manger in a little chapel where St. Ignatius of Loyola said his first Mass (I said a prayer there just for you and your family); Santa Croce with its holy nails and chunks of the True Cross. This was my first visit to La Scala Santa, the stairs Jesus climbed in Pilate's compound in Jerusalem (St. Helen brought all of it back in the 5th Century.) Anyway, the stairs are wood paved over in marble now for honor's sake, but there are places where you can see through glass to blood on the wood below and other places where you can reach through and touch the wood. It's customary to climb them on one's knees.

I wonder what you think of all this? I know it's hard to believe that things like a manger would last this long. But then I think about some of the things I've saved since I was little-- shells and scraps of letters; some of the things that have come down in the family like a cradle my great great great grandfather built. How much more likely would people be to treasure the cradle of Christ?

The story of your mother's miracle came often to my mind as we passed the countless crutches left behind at healing sites. They made me think of a possible answer to your problem concerning Francis (I'll concede, for the moment, that word you used, "problem," but I really think you should consider it more in terms of mystery). Do you remember the story of the crippled man from the Gospel? The one whose friends lowered him through the roof to meet Jesus? The Gospel says that Jesus, seeing *their* faith, healed him. Maybe if Jesus sees your faith, that will be enough of a space for him to heal Francis. And that's the real thing to keep in mind--in the end, it's not your job to heal Francis. One of the hardest things in the world is realizing that we're not God and that we can't save the people we love by ourselves. Have faith that God will be God and will heal as he sees fit. In the meantime, just be Francis's friend and do your best to be faithful for him. I know this isn't the easiest advice-- it's easy to feel that we're never doing enough and even easier to feel that we can do everything if we really want. You're not alone, though. We never are.

Well, it's getting late, and I don't want to bore you, so I'll leave off for now. Daddy's charmed by my account of you-- would you like to come visit us at some point over the Christmas holidays? He'll be home for a few weeks and wants to meet you. Let me know what you think. Meanwhile know that you're in my prayers, and I trust I'll be in yours.

Con affetto,

Molly

Roman had cooled sufficiently during his reading to recline comfortably on a couch. He now dropped the letter to his lap, looked to the ceiling, and followed a thin crack from the fireplace masonry toward the kitchen, where it splintered into gashes running to a ragged tear in the sheetrock. He still refused to think of his problem or mystery or whatever it was and mulled, for some time, over the images strewn about her letter, forming of each one a picture with which he would one day compare the ideas contained therein. The thought of visiting Molly of course excited him, but a Sicilian skepticism drew him immediately to the difficulties of acting upon such a proposal, mostly in the form of his parents, who no doubt would not only mistrust his visiting a girl but also wouldn't be pleased with his missing any time with them. Soon, though, tired and comfortably cool once more, he drifted into sleep thick with dreams.

He sat in what seemed a large room, the walls of something like adobe or light stone as he had once seen at Mesa Verde after the morning of the wild horses. The room stretched some thirty yards from where he sat near one of the walls. All seemed older here, faces especially. Old men, cheeks bearded, smooth, and brown, sat sleeping here and there in chunks of sun around the room, their feet twitching occasionally, their mouths twisting up into grins as if in pleasant dreams. Women and younger men peddled their wares quietly, their eyes dark and creased with close effort. Strong children accustomed to the sun danced about, laughing and playing unfamiliar and mournful tunes on sweet-toned flutes and chanting in distant tongues. He himself felt for the first time what it is to be old, to bear burdens in the bones and deeper in the brain and deepest in the love somehow rejected. The roof of the room hung low except for above his head where it soared as over an altar and vanished almost immediately into depthless darkness and he sensed that this darkness would forever ceil his experience. From the darkness there came a harder absence which nonetheless defined the space through which it passed and grew to seem like light.

And then from the darkness there appeared a hand, one he had often seen but now beheld transfigured. At first he saw only the tips of the fingers, and from each one there hung a drop of bright blood, and from the blood his eyes rose and found the palm wounded as if with many lips, and at the petalled center sat a fly, black and silent; and his eyes rose still until again a green eye absorbed him, and then a voice came to him, saying, "Why have you left me alone, Roman?"

"Francis?"

"If only you'd taken my hand, Roman, I could have rested. How will I rest now? How will I rest alone?"

Then the darkness was all for a moment until before him loomed a golden brilliance. Slowly he discerned the form of a tabernacle at the height of a man's chest. Silently its doors swung out and within, ringed with thorns, there beat a heart.

At each palpitant stroke the blood came bright and fresh against a green barb.

The heart was just before his eyes now and at an impulse he bent his lips to it. The blood was sweet to his tongue and soon it blended with his own blood, burning on his skin. His eyes were shut, though he felt the ticking of a thorn against the right lid and in his ears beat the heart like the sea in sleep as his own blood rushed quick and more quickly. Then the doors were shut and in their burnished faces he beheld darkly his own tattered visage and sensed a sudden warmth for himself.

At a sudden knock he opened his eyes. Cool and refreshed he yet struggled to attend. Again the knock. He had thought in the dullness of his waking that perhaps a package had arrived but now, aware of his loneliness, he crept to a window, slipping again into his sweatpants. The beating in his throat hardened at the sight of a man, perhaps thirty, looking down the balcony for signs of occupancy. His manner suggested familiarity with the place, and it was the notice of this alone that stilled Roman's urge to race upstairs for a gun. He stepped to the door. "Who is it?"

"It's Henry--my parents own this place."

Slowly, with much deliberation about the lock, Roman opened the door. The man stepped onto the foyer's wood floor, smiling. His teeth were yellow in the natural light.

"Thought nobody'd be here right now. My mom wanted me to pick something up for her."

"Yeah, I stayed home sick today."

"Well hey, feel better soon," and the man laid a soft hand on Roman's shoulder as he passed toward the door of the master bedroom. He had not at any moment met Roman's eye.

A little confused and more than a bit embarrassed, Roman loitered in the living room. Turning about he noticed that each of the seven lamps in the room was lit, the chains swinging slightly in chorus as the man clumped about. He had evidently begun shuffling papers, and Roman moved into the doorway to watch him. The man was hunched above a blue plastic container, and Roman, feeling more and more that something untoward was underway, stepped closer, saying, "Can I help you find something?" He glanced as he moved at a set of papers fanned on the bedspread. They were certainly his parents'.

The man started and turned his head. Roman stopped, pierced by the sudden blue of his eyes. "Where have you put it?" the man asked, the words immediate but each clearly pronounced.

"What are you talking about? These are my parents' things."

"This is my parents' house! They take you in and you move their things?" He was on his feet now, and almost without any interval he had taken Roman by the shoulders and shaken him. His breath bore an overwhelming scent of roses and through it cut the coppery voice in whispered shouts, "Where is the heart? Where is the heart?"

He woke then, startled, chill with sweat and disturbed by his mind's troubled pageantry. The light said some time had passed and looking at the clock between the bookshelves he saw that it was nearly four and that his mother would soon be home. Hastily he dressed and scribbled a note to the effect that he was going to the woods. Then he found Michael's pellet gun, a gift for his birthday, which had fallen in the previous week, and raced from the house, heart pounding at the possibility of capture and the conversation which could now no longer be avoided. The Sun was behind him as he strode toward and past the pond. A crow sat near the top of a maple tree, its leaves crisp and blood-bright in the cold, and the light set the crow's wings to flame as it noticed Roman and rose and beat its way, croaking coarsely, toward its forest redoubt. The light revealed the forest as from below as Roman completed his approach, and he knew that he, too, must be brightly visible until he had found the shadows. He stepped behind the trunk of a tall, thick pine just as he heard the tires on the dirt and yellow stones, and peering back he saw the grey Suburban shuffling up the drive. With a brief pang he remembered that he hadn't locked the door and would no doubt hear of his responsibility toward the home's owners later, but for the moment he again pushed the thought aside and pressed on into the woods.

He and Michael had gone this way perhaps two dozen times in the five days they'd lived on the property, and their path lay legible to any literate eye. They'd not yet scarred the bark of the fallen pine or stripped the fern fronds in their grasping passage, but here and there a chipped trunk or a trampled tendril belied their regular way, and the smaller animals had already modified their courses to accommodate them.

The air was still within the compass of the limbs, and cooler of course than near the pond. The trees thickened near the wood's far edge and then thinned abruptly into the cedar brush which had become for Roman the picture of lovely land. Ahead of him he saw the moon now just above the distant band of pines, and the thick meadow seemed in that hour to exist in tones of silver and pink, each feather, berry, and leaf softened and accented in the borrowed day.

Roman paused and watched and it softened and pressed upon him more sharply still. Then he pulled a pellet from his pocket, broke the barrel of the rifle with a crack of his palm, pressed the pellet into the barrel, snapped it shut, and began to hunt. He moved slowly, picking each step to soften its fall while looking hard around him for the slight signs which might reveal the presence of game before his own was revealed: the squirrel's barely waving branch, the chuckling flight of mourning doves or their soft coo. Crows called sharply far to his right. Behind him a mockingbird began his evening concert. Pistol shots popped steadily in the distance.

Ahead and to his left he noticed a pair of doves perched in a low pine, their grey breasts tinged in pink iridescence in the gathering dusk. A stand of grey, stunted tallow trees lay between him and them, and he crept through this gnarled arbor toward his prey, finally crawling on his belly through the dead leaves until he lay within twenty yards of the now somewhat wary birds. He saw by their sudden pacing and craning that he had caught their notice, so he aimed as quickly as he could without startling them (though he had always been slow with a rifle) and fired as the crosshairs settled on one of the grey breasts.

The wings' silvery beat began and he knew that at least one had flown away. He hurried to the ground below their perch and searched for the bird or feathers or blood. No sign presented itself and he accepted with irritation and embarrassment that he had shot badly. He glanced back at the dulled gleam of gold in the West and then pushed on, almost running away from the sun's setting. He had always found dusk a difficult time, a terrible time foreboding sickness and dolor in the dark, and he raced on to do something before the dark should fully fall.

His mind moved to the shallow stream in the ravine, and he made for it swiftly as he could. Needing to keep quiet and to steady his breath and his heart if another shot should come, though he felt the slimness of that chance, he slowed as he approached the steep and sudden slope and crept on hands and knees to its edge. He studied the banks in both directions, hoping to spy some dabbling ducks or some rabbits down for water before their evening feeding. He saw nothing but the minnows who cast no substantial shadows now and a thin snake, black, slithering up the still warm sand and vanishing into the bank.

He slid down the bank now and studied the stream's course. To his right it flowed into willow and darkened in descending into nearby pines. To his left it rose in clear sheets over the white sand out of a bend in its bed. The light seemed stronger there and there he went, picking his way silently, hugging the wall of the ravine, careful to avoid the spiders' evening spinnings. He came to the curve in the stream and still, as more and more of its course came clearly to his eye, no game showed itself. The anticipation which had swelled swiftly in him and hardened in his failure dissipated slowly and painfully, as if by a puncture so small as to go undetected.

He sat down on a large flat stone--ill-camouflaged, he thought--not so much to hunt as to prolong a little the time until he must return. A crowd of thoughts began to press upon him, to fill him with a dull dread by tomorrow's ever-greater imminence which seemed to fill him with a sickly anticipation which entered by hope's egress. His belly began to burn with worry.

Suddenly from before him came a snatch as of song or its beginning. Looking up to a low cedar bush on the rim of the ravine, he saw a small grey bird which by the black decurvity of its beak and the black mask across its eyes called him back from the ravine to the basement of memory, back to the space below the oak and the litter of leaves shot here and there with the flame of fallen feathers, back to the sudden sibilance which had drawn his eyes up to the same black mask upon the neighbor's chain fence and to the green anole below, pierced upon the crossed links. All that had begun to scatter and fade now sharpened and focused on that flecked breast and he imagined that he saw in it the dribblings of its kills. He planted his left foot on a raised stone in front of him, rested his left elbow on his elevated knee, and looked into the scope, still wobbling slightly, and this time he took care, guiding the body's infinitesimal tremblings through tightening gyres about the heart. And when the spiral, down, down, down through the sudden cold flesh reached its center, he pulled the trigger and the ravine grew silent again.

He sat for a moment, released the breath he'd unknowingly held, watched it stream out onto the now definitely cold air, then picked his way by large stones across the creek and climbed the ravine's opposite side, leaving the gun to rest against the clay bank.

He reached the lip, looked toward the cedar, saw the bird at its base. As his gaze sharpened, the triumph which had leapt up lightly inside him sank swiftly as if with a stone around its neck. The bird, a loggerhead shrike, he now remembered, had fallen on its side, one wing splayed, feathers rumpled. The red of the entry wound eclipsed the brown specklings of the breast. The legs bent out at freakish angles. A sudden horror struck Roman there in the gloom, and he drew backward, feeling too late his mistake as he tumbled into the gulch.

Before he could consider the rocks and roots below, he'd landed on his side in the sand. Yet before he could feel relief, the terror continued to swell up around him. He recognized now a sinister harmony in all of his being, the suddenly prime sostenuto that had held throughout the day below his impious improvisation in attempted distraction. With it came the deep commands he had heard the day before, calling from a cold center of the world. It rushed on him now, ravaged him, called up all reserves of the fear and anger he'd felt for Francis, Ruggi, Spencer, most of all himself and the divine cowardice by which he had conducted his friendships. He wept bitterly, breathlessly, fists and teeth tightening, trembling with utter loneliness and with anger, too, at this song whose sense maintained what seemed an utter invulnerability.

A sound broke upon his madness. The senses still touched his blazing mind and slowly he realized the sound's familiarity. He looked up and there, in the cedar, just visible in the dying dusk, stood another shrike. So strange did this seem that he paused, shook himself within, wondering, remembering with certainty his killing's accomplishment. Still the bird perched and sang. He watched it some seconds longer and then, noting again the growing gloom, turned for the house. His father was doubtless home by now, and he cast a half-embarrassed glance around, afraid to find searching eyes upon him.

The moon had risen definitely, and the last rays of the sun were slipping from the upper air to unveil the brightest of the stars. The silver lambence lit the lanes among cedar and tallow enough for him to walk without stumbling. All bore a closer examination then, the light of each life less harsh to his eyes. He saw the spiders' webs suspended as unsupported between the naked grey limbs, and the spiders held no fear for him then.

He reached the band of pines, heard the horned owls hooting in the cold quiet as he picked his steps calmly along the well-known way. Still the moon shone through here and there in bright pools, and he thought again of the owls and imagined, wildly, the mice of the pine floor waltzing in these silver drops.

He ducked beneath and slid once more over the fallen pine and found himself at the shore of the pond. He skirted its edge and passed beneath the great oak that shouldered its far bank. The light at his feet brightened as he stepped out of the shade and, looking behind him, saw the moon lying in the still water. He stopped, turned fully, and looked for some moments at the moon itself, now hanging clearly above the pines.

As he gazed he felt a fresh music beginning within him, fresh as only the eternal can be in its always having been. It was a borrowed song, a song of uncreated light, soothing yet wild and hot with the flame, if only echoed, of light's birth in the the dying heart of the sun, of the sun's birth in the burning heart of the world. And here again he prayed as if for the first time.

He did not know of all the rest who heard this song and reveled with him in its melody, of the farmer in the fields beyond the wood who loved his fallow land again, of the black dog in his nightly sortie against the raccoons rummaging in the garbage, of his mother on the porch seeing him in the light and knowing he had begun to hear.

He turned again toward the house, more slowly, though not now in sadness or shame, and he smiled as he climbed the steps and met his mother.

"Feeling better?" she asked, and before her he stepped into the living room just as Michael, racing ritually around, lit the seventh lamp and the seventh chain joined in the pendent descent to rest.

.

Made in USA - Kendallville, IN
1053857_9781952464003
03.17.2020 0827